A. S. PUSHKIN

The Queen of Spades

The Captain's Daughter

Translated by
GILLON R. AITKEN
Etchings by
CLARKE HUTTON

THE FOLIO SOCIETY
London 1970

The text of this edition is used by kind permission of
Barrie & Rockliff (Barrie Books Ltd)

PRINTED IN GREAT BRITAIN

Printed and bound by W & J Mackay & Co. Ltd, Chatham
Set in Walbaum 12 Didot on 13 point body
Illustrations printed by Kultura, Budapest

For Ann

Contents and Illustrations

INTRODUCTION *page* 5

THE QUEEN OF SPADES *page* 9

Lisaveta Ivanovna began to look out of the
    window   *facing page* 18

Before the Countess stood an unknown man   32

Hermann merely mutters: 'Three, seven, ace!
    Three, seven, queen!'   47

THE CAPTAIN'S DAUGHTER *page* 49

Marya Ivanovna entered the room (p.79) *frontispiece*

My guide winked significantly   *facing page* 69

When I awoke Marya Ivanovna was standing
    before me   96

The moon was lighting up the gallows   133

On the floor sat Marya Ivanovna   164

Introduction

Pushkin holds the supreme position in Russian literature. It was his genius which created, in the fullest
sense, a national literature, and which laid the foun-
dations upon which that literature could subsequently
be built. Until his emergence at the beginning of the
nineteenth century, writing in Russia, with the
exception of a handful of works, had been mainly
imitative, pursuing pseudo-classical principles and
reflecting closely the trends of various Western
European cultures – French, in particular. The
lyrical simplicity and precision of Pushkin's poetry,
the natural, straightforward grace of his prose per-
fectly expressed the Russian mood; and, in that
expression, Pushkin gave to Russia for the first time
in her history a literature whose inspiration came
from herself. But his achievements were more than
national: his universality of vision, his ability to
transmute what he saw and what he understood into
language of the utmost purity and point have created
for him a permanent place in the literature of the
world.

Alexandr Sergeyevitch Pushkin was born in Moscow on 26 May 1799. On his father's side, he was of
ancient boyar stock; on his mother's side, and as his
physical appearance hinted at, he was descended from
an Abyssinian Prince whose son was taken from his
father as a hostage and later presented to the Emperor
Peter the Great.

Pushkin's early childhood was unremarkable. He
was brought up in a literary household – both his
father and his uncle wrote verse – but the influence

of his parents was a remote one. Stronger, certainly, was that of his nurse, Anna Rodionovna, who was glad to impart her wide knowledge of Russian folklore and who instilled in him a deep love of the Russian language. As a counter to the effect of the widespread usage of the French language in Russia, Anna Rodionovna's place in Pushkin's life is important: in educated circles, French was the language of the day; Pushkin received a primarily French education, and his early reading – by the age of ten, he was a voracious reader, and he remained one – was drawn from his father's excellent French library.

At the age of twelve, Pushkin was sent to the Lyceum at Tsarskoye Selo. He remained there six years. Discipline was lax, and, in an atmosphere of freedom, his poetic instinct was quick to show itself. He wrote first in French, then in Russian. By 1814, his poems had begun to be printed; by the time he left the Lyceum and went to St Petersburg in 1817, Pushkin had already been acclaimed as a 'new voice'. Derzhavin, Zhukovsky, Karamzin, eminent writers of an older generation, were among the first to recognize in the ease and fluency of Pushkin's early verse the careless quality of genius.

In 1820, Pushkin was exiled by the Tsar Alexander I for his part in a 'liberal' movement against the government. His exile lasted over five years, spent mostly in Southern Russia – at Ekaterinoslav, at Kishinev, at Odessa. It was a period in which his poetic genius flowered, in which he grew to maturity. He became aware of the richness and diversity of his gifts. He responded to new influences – the Crimea, the Caucasus. With the leisure that exile entailed, he learned English and Italian; he 'discovered' Byron, who opened up a new world to him and left a lasting impression.

Pushkin's output was prodigious during these years: he wrote two long poems in the Byronic manner, *The Prisoner of the Caucasus* and *The Bakhchisarai Fountain*, numerous lyrics and ballads, a further long poem, *The Gypsies*, which had a considerable popular success; in addition, he completed *Boris Godunov*, a play based on the story of 'false' Demetrius, and he began the masterpiece for which he is best known, *Eugene Onegin*, a vivid 'novel' in verse of great technical brilliance and virtuosity.

Pushkin completed the final canto of *Eugene Onegin* in 1831; at once a story of the emotions and a picture of contemporary Russian life, it is his most important work, a work of perfection by which, if he had written nothing else, his reputation would be uniquely assured. Thereafter, prose was to concern him more than verse.

In 1829, on his return from a second visit to the Caucasus, Pushkin had become engaged to Natalya Goncharova, a young society beauty. His engagement, although not a cause of it, marked a turning-point in his life: until the age of thirty, he was hot-headed and passionate, a 'liberal' who incurred the disapproval of both church and state; his work had been subjected to constant censorship – even the personal censorship of Tsar Nicholas I, who had succeeded Alexander a few months before the ill-fated Decembrists' Revolt, with which Pushkin was incidentally involved, in 1825. After he was thirty, and particularly after his marriage in 1831, he began to 'conform': he had grown more serious; the effects of censorship had been wearying. This turning-point coincided with his earlier prose writing.

In 1836, Pushkin received an anonymous letter suggesting that his wife was having a love affair with a Baron d'Anthes. He was persuaded to withdraw his

challenge to d'Anthes to a pistol duel. Fresh insinuations made a duel inevitable, however. It took place on
27 January 1837. D'Anthes was slightly wounded;
Pushkin received injuries which proved fatal, and he
died on 29 January at the age of thirty-seven.

This volume contains the two prose tales by which
Pushkin is chiefly remembered: *The Queen of Spades*
and *The Captain's Daughter*. He wrote much else
besides – *Dubrovsky*, an unfinished work of near novel
length; *The Tales of the late Ivan Petrovitch Belkin*,
notable for the picture they give of Russian provincial
life of the time; *The Moor of Peter the Great*, based on
the life of Pushkin's mother's grandfather; and five
shorter pieces.

The Queen of Spades was published in 1834. It is
certainly Pushkin's most successful prose work of a
short kind – indeed, it is one of the greatest short
stories in world literature: scarcely more than 10,000
words in length, brilliantly compressed, written with
great vividness, it achieves an altogether unforgettable
effect.

The Captain's Daughter, the longest of Pushkin's
completed prose tales, was written between 1833 and
1836. Based on true events which Pushkin wrote as
history in his *The History of the Pugachev Rebellion*,
it is a masterpiece of writing and construction. It is
memorable not only for the thrilling account it offers
of the exploits of a peasant brigand, Pugachev, in his
attempt to overthrow the Empress Catherine II, but
also for the valuable impressions it offers of army life
in a remote garrison town in Southern Russia.

The two tales printed here represent the best of
Pushkin's prose writing, and are to be ranked among
the finest in the Russian language.

GILLON R. AITKEN

The Queen of Spades

The Queen of Spades signifies a secret misfortune.

FROM A RECENT BOOK ON
FORTUNE-TELLING

Chapter One

And on rainy days
They gathered
Often;
Their stakes – God help them! –
Wavered from fifty
To a hundred,
And they won
And marked up their winnings
With chalk.
Thus on rainy days
Were they
*Busy.**

There was a card party one day in the rooms of Narumov, an officer of the Horse Guards. The long winter
evening slipped by unnoticed; it was five o'clock in the
morning before the assembly sat down to supper. Those
who had won ate with a big appetite; the others sat
distractedly before their empty plates. But champagne
was brought in, the conversation became more lively,
and everyone took a part in it.

'And how did you get on, Surin?' asked the host.

'As usual, I lost. I must confess, I have no luck: I
never vary my stake, never get heated, never lose my
head, and yet I always lose!'

'And weren't you tempted even once to back on a
series . . ? Your strength of mind astonishes me.'

'What about Hermann then,' said one of the guests,
pointing at the young Engineer. 'He's never held a
card in his hand, never doubled a single stake in his
life, and yet he sits up until five in the morning watching us play.'

'The game fascinates me,' said Hermann, 'but I am

* From a letter by Pushkin to Vyazemsky.

not in the position to sacrifice the essentials of life in the hope of acquiring the luxuries.'

'Hermann's a German: he's cautious – that's all,' Tomsky observed. 'But if there's one person I can't understand, it's my grandmother, the Countess Anna Fedotovna.'

'How? Why?' the guests inquired noisily.

'I can't understand why it is,' Tomsky continued, 'that my grandmother doesn't gamble.'

'But what's so astonishing about an old lady of eighty not gambling?' asked Narumov.

'Then you don't know . . ?'

'No, indeed; I know nothing.'

'Oh well, listen then:

'You must know that about sixty years ago my grandmother went to Paris, where she made something of a hit. People used to chase after her to catch a glimpse of *la vénus moscovite*; Richelieu paid court to her, and my grandmother vouches that he almost shot himself on account of her cruelty. At that time ladies used to play faro.* On one occasion at the Court, my grandmother lost a very great deal of money on credit to the Duke of Orleans.† Returning home, she removed the patches from her face, took off her hooped petticoat, announced her loss to my grandfather and ordered him to pay back the money. My late grandfather, as far as I can remember, was a sort of lackey to my grandmother. He feared her like fire; on hearing of such a disgraceful loss, however, he completely lost his temper; he produced his accounts, showed her that she had spent half a million francs in six months,

---

* A game of pure chance, at which the players gamble on the order in which certain cards will appear when taken singly from the top of the pack. The stakes are placed on one or more of a suit of spades lying on the table.

† Louis Philippe (1725–85), grandson of the Regent of France.

pointed out that neither their Moscow nor their Sara-
tov estates were in Paris, and refused point-blank to
pay the debt. My grandmother gave him a box on the
ear and went off to sleep on her own as an indication of
her displeasure. In the hope that this domestic inflic-
tion would have had some effect on him, she sent for
her husband the next day; she found him unshakable.
For the first time in her life she approached him with
argument and explanation, thinking that she could
bring him to reason by pointing out that there are
debts and debts, that there is a big difference between
a Prince and a coach-maker. But my grandfather
remained adamant, and flatly refused to discuss the
subject any further. My grandmother did not know
what to do. A little while before, she had become
acquainted with a very remarkable man. You have
heard of Count St-Germain,* about whom so many
marvellous stories are related. You know that he held
himself out to be the Wandering Jew, and the inventor
of the elixir of life, the philosopher's stone and so forth.
Some ridiculed him as a charlatan and in his memoirs
Casanova† declares that he was a spy. However,
St-Germain, in spite of the mystery which surrounded
him, was a person of venerable appearance and much
in demand in society. My grandmother is still quite
infatuated with him and becomes quite angry if anyone
speaks of him with disrespect. My grandmother knew
that he had large sums of money at his disposal. She
decided to have recourse to him, and wrote asking him
to visit her without delay. The eccentric old man at
once called on her and found her in a state of terrible
grief. She depicted her husband's barbarity in the

* Died about 1795: reckoned by some as an impostor, by others
as endowed with mystical powers.
† Casanova de Seingalt (1725–98), a fashionable adventurer,
known for his scandalous memoirs.

blackest light, and ended by saying that she pinned all her hopes on his friendship and kindness.

'St-Germain reflected. "I could let you have this sum," he said, "but I know that you would not be at peace while in my debt, and I have no wish to bring fresh troubles upon your head. There is another solution – you can win back the money."

' "But, my dear Count," my grandmother replied, "I tell you – we have no money at all."

' "In this case money is not essential," St-Germain replied. "Be good enough to hear me out."

'And at this point he revealed to her the secret for which any one of us here would give a great deal . . .'

The young gamblers listened with still greater attention. Tomsky lit his pipe, drew on it and continued:

'That same evening my grandmother went to Versailles, *au jeu de la Reine*. The Duke of Orleans kept the bank; inventing some small tale, my grandmother lightly excused herself for not having brought her debt, and began to play against him. She chose three cards and played them one after the other: all three won and my grandmother recouped herself completely.'

'Pure luck!' said one of the guests.

'A fairy-tale,' observed Hermann.

'Perhaps the cards were marked!' said a third.

'I don't think so,' Tomsky replied gravely.

'What!' cried Narumov. 'You have a grandmother who can guess three cards in succession, and you haven't yet contrived to learn her secret.'

'No, not much hope of that!' replied Tomsky. 'She had four sons, including my father; all four were desperate gamblers, and yet she did not reveal her secret to a single one of them, although it would have been a good thing if she had told them – told me, even. But this is what I heard from my uncle, Count

Ivan Ilyitch, and he gave me his word for its truth. The late Chaplitsky – the same who died a pauper after squandering millions – in his youth once lost nearly 300,000 roubles – to Zoritch, if I remember rightly. He was in despair. My grandmother, who was most strict in her attitude towards the extravagances of young men, for some reason took pity on Chaplitsky. She told him the three cards on condition that he played them in order; and at the same time she exacted his solemn promise that he would never play again as long as he lived. Chaplitsky appeared before his victor; they sat down to play. On the first card Chaplitsky staked 50,000 roubles and won straight off; he doubled his stake, redoubled – and won back more than he had lost . . .

'But it's time to go to bed; it's already a quarter to six.'

Indeed, the day was already beginning to break. The young men drained their glasses and dispersed.

Chapter Two

'Il paraît que monsieur est décidément
pour les suivantes.'
'Que voulez-vous, madame? Elles sont
plus fraîches.'

FASHIONABLE CONVERSATION

The old Countess *** was seated before the looking-glass in her dressing-room. Three lady's maids stood by her. One held a jar of rouge, another a box of hairpins, and the third a tall bonnet with flame-coloured ribbons. The Countess no longer had the slightest pretensions to beauty, which had long since faded from her face, but she still preserved all the habits of her youth, paid strict regard to the fashions of the seventies, and devoted to her dress the same time and attention as she had done sixty years before. At an embroidery frame by the window sat a young lady, her ward.

'Good morning, *grand'maman*!' said a young officer as he entered the room. '*Bonjour, mademoiselle Lise. Grand'maman*, I have a request to make of you.'

'What is it, Paul?'

'I want you to let me introduce one of my friends to you, and to allow me to bring him to the ball on Friday.'

'Bring him straight to the ball and introduce him to me there. Were you at ***'s yesterday?'

'Of course. It was very gay; we danced until five in the morning. How charming Eletskaya was!'

'But, my dear, what's charming about her? Isn't she like her grandmother, the Princess Darya Petrovna . . ? By the way, I dare say she's grown very old now, the Princess Darya Petrovna?'

'What do you mean, "grown old"?' asked Tomsky thoughtlessly. 'She's been dead for seven years.'

The young lady raised her head and made a sign to the young man. He remembered then that the death of any of her contemporaries was kept secret from the old Countess, and he bit his lip. But the Countess heard the news, previously unknown to her, with the greatest indifference.

'Dead!' she said. 'And I didn't know it. We were maids of honour together, and when we were presented, the Empress . . .'

And for the hundredth time the Countess related the anecdote to her grandson.

'Come, Paul,' she said when she had finished her story, 'help me to stand up. Lisanka, where's my snuff-box?'

And with her three maids the Countess went behind a screen to complete her dress. Tomsky was left alone with the young lady.

'Whom do you wish to introduce?' Lisaveta Ivanovna asked softly.

'Narumov. Do you know him?'

'No. Is he a soldier or a civilian?'

'A soldier.'

'An Engineer?'

'No, he's in the Cavalry. What made you think he was an Engineer?'

The young lady smiled but made no reply.

'Paul!' cried the Countess from behind the screen. 'Bring along a new novel with you some time, will you, only please not one of those modern ones.'

'What do you mean, *grand'maman*?'

'I mean not the sort of novel in which the hero strangles either of his parents or in which someone is drowned. I have a great horror of drowned people.'

'Such novels don't exist nowadays. Wouldn't you like a Russian one?'

'Are there such things? Send me one, my dear, please send me one.'

'Will you excuse me now, *grand'maman*, I'm in a hurry. Good-bye, Lisaveta Ivanovna. What made you think that Narumov was in the Engineers?'

And Tomsky left the dressing-room.

Lisaveta Ivanovna was left on her own; she put aside her work and began to look out of the window. Presently a young officer appeared from behind the corner house on the other side of the street. A flush spread over her cheeks; she took up her work again and lowered her head over the frame. At this moment, the Countess returned, fully dressed.

'Order the carriage, Lisanka,' she said, 'and we'll go for a drive.'

Lisanka got up from behind her frame and began to put away her work.

'What's the matter with you, my child? Are you deaf?' shouted the Countess. 'Order the carriage this minute.'

'I'll do so at once,' the young lady replied softly and hastened into the ante-room.

A servant entered the room and handed the Countess some books from the Prince Pavel Alexandrovitch.

'Good, thank him,' said the Countess. 'Lisanka, Lisanka, where are you running to?'

'To get dressed.'

'Plenty of time for that, my dear. Sit down. Open the first volume and read to me.'

The young lady took up the book and read a few lines.

'Louder!' said the Countess. 'What's the matter with you, my child? Have you lost your voice, or what . . ? Wait . . . move that footstool up to me . . . nearer . . . that's right!'

Lisaveta Ivanovna read a further two pages. The Countess yawned.

'Put the book down,' she said; 'what rubbish! Have it returned to Prince Pavel with my thanks. . . . But where is the carriage?'

'The carriage is ready,' said Lisaveta Ivanovna, looking out into the street.

'Then why aren't you dressed?' asked the Countess. I'm always having to wait for you – it's intolerable, my dear!'

Lisa ran up to her room. Not two minutes elapsed before the Countess began to ring with all her might. The three lady's maids came running in through one door and the valet through another.

'Why don't you come when you're called?' the Countess asked them. 'Tell Lisaveta Ivanovna that I'm waiting for her.'

Lisaveta Ivanovna entered the room wearing her hat and cloak.

'At last, my child!' said the Countess. 'But what clothes you're wearing . . .! Whom are you hoping to catch? What's the weather like? It seems windy.'

'There's not a breath of wind, your Ladyship,' replied the valet.

'You never know what you're talking about! Open that small window. There; as I thought: windy and bitterly cold. Unharness the horses. Lisaveta, we're not going out – there was no need to dress up like that.'

'And this is my life,' thought Lisaveta Ivanovna.

And indeed Lisaveta Ivanovna was a most unfortunate creature. As Dante says: 'You shall learn the salt taste of another's bread, and the hard path up and down his stairs';* and who better to know the bitterness of dependence than the poor ward of a well-born old lady? The Countess *** was far from being wicked, but she had the capriciousness of a woman who has been spoiled by the world, and the miserliness and

* *Paradiso*, xvii. 58.

cold-hearted egotism of all old people who have done with loving and whose thoughts lie with the past. She took part in all the vanities of the *haut monde*; she dragged herself to balls, where she sat in a corner, rouged and dressed in old-fashioned style, like some misshapen but essential ornament of the ball-room; on arrival, the guests would approach her with low bows, as if in accordance with an established rite, but after that, they would pay no further attention to her. She received the whole town at her house, and although no longer able to recognize the faces of her guests, she observed the strictest etiquette. Her numerous servants, grown fat and grey in her hall and servants' room did exactly as they pleased, vying with one another in stealing from the dying old lady. Lisaveta Ivanovna was the household martyr. She poured out the tea, and was reprimanded for putting in too much sugar; she read novels aloud, and was held guilty of all the faults of the authors; she accompanied the Countess on her walks, and was made responsible for the state of the weather and the pavement. There was a salary attached to her position, but it was never paid; meanwhile, it was demanded of her to be dressed like everybody else – that is, like the very few who could afford to dress well. In society she played the most pitiable role. Everybody knew her, but nobody took any notice of her; at balls she danced only when there was a partner short, and ladies only took her arm when they needed to go to the dressing-room to make some adjustment to their dress. She was proud and felt her position keenly, and looked around her in impatient expectation of a deliverer; but the young men, calculating in their flightiness, did not honour her with their attention, despite the fact that Lisaveta Ivanovna was a hundred times prettier than the cold, arrogant but more eligible young ladies on whom they danced attendance. Many a time did she creep softly away from the bright but wearisome drawing-room to go and cry in her own poor room, where stood a papered screen, a chest of drawers, a small looking-glass and a painted bedstead, and where a tallow candle burned dimly in its copper candle-stick.

One day – two days after the evening described at the beginning of this story, and about a week previous to the events just recorded – Lisaveta Ivanovna was sitting at her embroidery frame by the window, when, happening to glance out into the street, she saw a young Engineer, standing motionless with his eyes fixed upon her window. She lowered her head and continued with her work; five minutes later she looked out again – the young officer was still standing in the same place. Not being in the habit of flirting with passing officers, she ceased to look out of the window, and sewed for about two hours without raising her head. Dinner was announced. She got up and began to put away her frame, and, glancing casually out into the street, she saw the officer again. She was considerably puzzled by this. After dinner, she approached the window with a feeling of some disquiet, but the officer was no longer outside, and she thought no more of him.

Two days later, while preparing to enter the carriage with the Countess, she saw him again. He was standing just by the front door, his face concealed by a beaver collar; his dark eyes shone from beneath his cap. Without knowing why, Lisaveta Ivanovna felt afraid, and an unaccountable trembling came over her as she sat down in the carriage.

On her return home, she hastened to the window – the officer was standing in the same place as before, his eyes fixed upon her; she drew back, tormented by curiosity and agitated by a feeling that was quite new to her.

Since then, not a day had passed without the young man appearing at the customary hour beneath the window of their house. A sort of mute acquaintance grew up between them. At work in her seat, she used to feel him approaching, and would raise her head to look at him – for longer and longer each day. The young man seemed to be grateful to her for this: she saw, with the sharp eye of youth, how a sudden flush would spread across his pale cheeks on each occasion that their glances met. After a week she smiled at him . . .

When Tomsky asked leave of the Countess to introduce one of his friends to her, the poor girl's heart beat fast. But on learning that Narumov was in the Horse Guards, and not in the Engineers, she was sorry that, by an indiscreet question, she had betrayed her secret to the light-hearted Tomsky.

Hermann was the son of a Russianized German, from whom he had inherited a small amount of money. Being firmly convinced of the necessity of ensuring his independence, Hermann did not draw on the income that this yielded, but lived on his pay, forbidding himself the slightest extravagance. Moreover, he was secretive and ambitious, and his companions rarely had occasion to laugh at his excessive thrift. He had strong passions and a fiery imagination, but his tenacity of spirit saved him from the usual errors of youth. Thus, for example, although at heart a gambler, he never took a card in his hand, for he reckoned that his position did not allow him (as he put it) 'to sacrifice the essentials of life in the hope of acquiring the luxuries' – and meanwhile, he would sit up at the card table for whole nights at a time, and follow the different turns of the game with feverish anxiety.

The story of the three cards had made a strong impression on his imagination, and he could think of nothing else all night.

'What if the old Countess should reveal her secret to me?' he thought the following evening as he wandered through the streets of Petersburg. 'What if she should tell me the names of those three winning cards? Why not try my luck . . ? Become introduced to her, try to win her favour, perhaps become her lover . . .? But all that demands time, and she's eighty-seven; she might die in a week, in two days . . ! And the story itself . . ? Can one really believe it . . ? No! Economy, moderation and industry; these are my three winning cards, these will treble my capital, increase it sevenfold, and earn for me ease and independence!'

Reasoning thus, he found himself in one of the principal streets of Petersburg, before a house of old-fashioned architecture. The street was crowded with vehicles; one after another, carriages rolled up to the lighted entrance. From them there emerged, now the shapely little foot of some beautiful young woman, now a rattling jack-boot, now the striped stocking and elegant shoe of a diplomat. Furs and capes flitted past the majestic hall-porter. Hermann stopped.

'Whose house is this?' he asked the watchman at the corner.

'The Countess ***'s,' the watchman replied.

Hermann started. His imagination was again fired by the amazing story of the three cards. He began to walk around near the house, thinking of its owner and her mysterious faculty. It was late when he returned to his humble rooms; for a long time he could not sleep, and when at last he did drop off, cards, a green table, heaps of banknotes and piles of golden coins appeared to him in his dreams. He played one card after the other, doubled his stake decisively, won unceasingly, and raked in the golden coins and stuffed his pockets with the banknotes. Waking up late, he sighed at the loss of his imaginary fortune, again went out to wander about the town and again found himself outside the house of the Countess * * *. Some unknown power seemed to have attracted him to it. He stopped and began to look at the windows. At one he saw a head with long black hair, probably bent down over a book or a piece of work. The head was raised. Hermann saw a small, fresh face and a pair of dark eyes. That moment decided his fate.

Chapter Three

Vous m'écrivez, mon ange, des lettres de
quatre page plus vite que je ne puis les lire.
CORRESPONDENCE

Scarcely had Lisaveta Ivanovna taken off her hat and cloak when the Countess sent for her and again ordered her to have the horses harnessed. They went out to take their seats in the carriage. At the same moment as the old lady was being helped through the carriage doors by two footmen, Lisaveta Ivanovna saw her Engineer standing close by the wheel; he seized her hand; before she could recover from her fright, the young man had disappeared – leaving a letter in her hand. She hid it in her glove and throughout the whole of her drive neither heard nor saw a thing. As was her custom when riding in her carriage, the Countess kept up a ceaseless flow of questions: 'Who was it who met us just now? What's this bridge called? What's written on that signboard?' This time Lisaveta Ivanovna's answers were so vague and inappropriate that the Countess became angry.

'What's the matter with you, my child? Are you in a trance or something? Don't you hear me or understand what I'm saying . . ? Heaven be thanked that I'm still sane enough to speak clearly.'

Lisaveta Ivanovna did not listen to her. On returning home, she ran up to her room and drew the letter out of her glove; it was unsealed. Lisaveta Ivanovna read it through. The letter contained a confession of love; it was tender, respectful and taken word for word from a German novel. But Lisaveta Ivanovna had no knowledge of German and was most pleased by it.

Nevertheless, the letter made her feel extremely uneasy. For the first time in her life she was entering into a secret and confidential relationship with a young man. His audacity shocked her. She reproached herself for her imprudent behaviour, and did not know what to do. Should she stop sitting at the window and by a show of indifference cool off the young man's desire for further acquaintance? Should she send the letter back to him? Or answer it with cold-hearted finality? There was nobody to whom she could turn for advice: she had no friend or preceptress. Lisaveta Ivanovna resolved to answer the letter.

She sat down at her small writing-table, took a pen and some paper, and lost herself in thought. Several times she began her letter – and then tore it up; her manner of expression seemed to her to be either too condescending or too heartless. At last she succeeded in writing a few lines that satisfied her:

I am sure that your intentions are honourable, and that you did not wish to offend me by your rash behaviour, but our acquaintance must not begin in this way. I return your letter to you and hope that in the future I shall have no cause to complain of undeserved disrespect.

The next day, as soon as she saw Hermann approach, Lisaveta Ivanovna rose from behind her frame, went into the ante-room, opened a small window, and threw her letter into the street, trusting to the agility of the young officer to pick it up. Hermann ran forward, took hold of the letter and went into a confectioner's shop. Breaking the seal of the envelope, he found his own letter and Lisaveta Ivanovna's answer. It was as he had expected, and he returned home, deeply preoccupied with his intrigue.

Three days afterwards, a bright-eyed young girl brought Lisaveta Ivanovna a letter from a milliner's shop. Lisaveta Ivanovna opened it uneasily, envisaging a demand for money, but she suddenly recognized Hermann's handwriting.

'You have made a mistake, my dear,' she said: 'this letter is not for me.'

'Oh, but it is!' the girl answered cheekily and without concealing a sly smile. 'Read it.'

Lisaveta Ivanovna ran her eyes over the note. Hermann demanded a meeting.

'It cannot be,' said Lisaveta Ivanovna, frightened at the haste of his demand and the way in which it was made: 'this is certainly not for me.'

And she tore the letter up into tiny pieces.

'If the letter wasn't for you, why did you tear it up?' asked the girl. 'I would have returned it to the person who sent it.'

'Please, my dear,' Lisaveta Ivanovna said, flushing at the remark, 'don't bring me any more letters in future. And tell the person who sent you that he should be ashamed of . . .'

But Hermann was not put off. By some means or other, he sent a letter to Lisaveta Ivanovna every day. The letters were no longer translated from the German. Hermann wrote them inspired by passion, and used a language true to his character; these letters were the expression of his obsessive desires and the disorder of his unfettered imagination. Lisaveta Ivanovna no longer thought of returning them to him: she revelled in them, began to answer them, and with each day, her replies became longer and more tender. Finally, she threw out of the window the following letter:

This evening there is a ball at the *** Embassy. The Countess will be there. We will stay until about two o'clock. Here is your chance to see me alone. As soon as

*the Countess has left the house, the servants will prob-
ably go to their quarters – with the exception of the
hall-porter, who normally goes out to his closet anyway. Come at half-past eleven. Walk straight upstairs.
If you meet anybody in the ante-room, ask whether the
Countess is at home. You will be told 'No' – and there
will be nothing you can do but go away. But it is unlikely
that you will meet anybody. The lady's maids sit by
themselves, all in the one room. On leaving the hall,
turn to the left and walk straight on until you come to
the Countess's bedroom. In the bedroom, behind a screen,
you will see two small doors: the one on the right leads
into the study, which the Countess never goes into; the
one on the left leads into a corridor and thence to a narrow winding staircase: this staircase leads to my bedroom.*

Hermann quivered like a tiger as he awaited the
appointed hour. He was already outside the Countess's
house at ten o'clock. The weather was terrible; the
wind howled, and a wet snow fell in large flakes upon
the deserted streets, where the lamps shone dimly.
Occasionally a passing cab-driver leaned forward over
his scrawny nag, on the look-out for a late passenger.
Feeling neither wind nor snow, Hermann waited,
dressed only in his frock-coat. At last the Countess's
carriage was brought round. Hermann saw two footmen carry out in their arms the bent old lady, wrapped
in a sable fur, and immediately following her, the
figure of Lisaveta Ivanovna, clad in a light cloak, and
with her head adorned with fresh flowers. The doors
were slammed and the carriage rolled heavily away
along the soft snow. The hall-porter closed the front
door. The windows became dark. Hermann began to
walk about near the deserted house; he went up to a
lamp and looked at his watch; it was twenty minutes

past eleven. He remained beneath the lamp, his eyes
fixed upon the hands of his watch, waiting for the
remaining minutes to pass. At exactly half-past eleven,
Hermann ascended the steps of the Countess's house
and reached the brightly-lit porch. The hall-porter
was not there. Hermann ran up the stairs, opened the
door into the ante-room and saw a servant asleep by the
lamp in a soiled antique armchair. With a light, firm
tread Hermann stepped past him. The drawing-room
and reception-room were in darkness, but the lamp in
the ante-room sent through a feeble light. Hermann
passed through into the bedroom. Before an icon case,
filled with old-fashioned images, glowed a gold sanctuary lamp. Faded brocade armchairs and dull gilt divans
with soft cushions were ranged in sad symmetry
around the room, the walls of which were hung with
Chinese silk. Two portraits, painted in Paris by Madame
Lebrun, * hung from one of the walls. One of these
featured a plump, red-faced man of about forty, in a
light-green uniform and with a star pinned to his
breast; the other – a beautiful young woman with an
aquiline nose and powdered hair, brushed back at the
temples and adorned with a rose. In the corners of the
room stood porcelain shepherdesses, table clocks from
the workshop of the celebrated Leroy,† little boxes,
roulettes, fans and the various lady's playthings which
had been popular at the end of the last century, when
the Montgolfiers' balloon‡ and Mesmer's magnetism§
were invented. Hermann went behind the screen,
where stood a small iron bedstead; on the right was the

* Elisabeth Vigée-Lebrun (1755–1842), famous French portrait
painter, for whom the Russian Imperial family sat.
† A well-known Parisian clock-maker.
‡ Joseph-Michel (1740–1810) and Jacques-Etienne Montgolfier
(1745–99), inventors of the hydrogen balloon.
§ Franz Anton Mesmer (1734–1815), Austrian doctor who founded
the theory of animal magnetism.

door leading to the study; on the left the one which led to the corridor. Hermann opened the latter, and saw the narrow, winding staircase which led to the poor ward's room . . . But he turned back and stepped into the dark study.

The time passed slowly. Everything was quiet. The clock in the drawing-room struck twelve; one by one the clocks in all the other rooms sounded the same hour, and then all was quiet again. Hermann stood leaning against the cold stove. He was calm; his heart beat evenly, like that of a man who has decided upon some dangerous but necessary action. One o'clock sounded; two o'clock; he heard the distant rattle of the carriage. He was seized by an involuntary agitation. The carriage drew near and stopped. He heard the sound of the carriage-steps being let down. The house suddenly came alive. Servants ran here and there, voices echoed through the house and the rooms were lit. Three old maid-servants hastened into the bed-room, followed by the Countess, who, tired to death, lowered herself into a Voltairean * armchair. Hermann peeped through a crack. Lisaveta Ivanovna went past him. Hermann heard her hurried steps as she went up the narrow staircase. In his heart there echoed something like the voice of conscience, but it grew silent, and his heart once more turned to stone.

The Countess began to undress before the looking-glass. Her rose-bedecked cap was unfastened; her powdered wig was removed from her grey, closely-cropped hair. Pins fell in showers around her. Her yellow dress, embroidered with silver, fell at her swollen feet. Hermann witnessed all the loathsome mysteries of her dress; at last the Countess stood in her dressing-gown and night-cap; in this attire, more suitable to her age, she seemed less hideous and revolting.

* A chair with a high winged back and a low seat.

Like most old people, the Countess suffered from insomnia. Having undressed, she sat down by the window in the Voltairean armchair and dismissed her maidservants. The candles were carried out; once again the room was lit by a single sanctuary lamp. Looking quite yellow, the Countess sat rocking to and fro in her chair, her flabby lips moving. Her dim eyes reflected a complete absence of thought and, looking at her, one would have thought that the awful old woman's rocking came not of her own volition, but by the action of some hidden galvanism.

Suddenly, an indescribable change came over her death-like face. Her lips ceased to move, her eyes came to life: before the Countess stood an unknown man.

'Don't be alarmed, for God's sake, don't be alarmed,' he said in a clear, low voice. 'I have no intention of harming you; I have come to beseech a favour of you.'

The old woman looked at him in silence, as if she had not heard him. Hermann imagined that she was deaf, and bending right down over her ear, he repeated what he had said. The old woman kept silent as before.

'You can ensure the happiness of my life,' Hermann continued, 'and it will cost you nothing: I know that you can guess three cards in succession. . . .'

Hermann stopped. The Countess appeared to understand what was demanded of her; she seemed to be seeking words for her reply.

'It was a joke,' she said at last. 'I swear to you, it was a joke.'

'There's no joking about it,' Hermann retorted angrily. 'Remember Chaplitsky whom you helped to win.'

The Countess was visibly disconcerted, and her features expressed strong emotion; but she quickly resumed her former impassivity.

'Can you name these three winning cards?' Hermann continued.

The Countess was silent. Hermann went on:

'For whom do you keep your secret? For your grandsons? They are rich and they can do without it; they don't know the value of money. Your three cards will not help a spendthrift. He who cannot keep his paternal inheritance will die in want, even if he has the devil at his side. I am not a spendthrift; I know the value of money. Your three cards will not be lost on me. Come . . !'

He stopped and awaited her answer with trepidation. The Countess was silent. Hermann fell upon his knees.

'If your heart has ever known the feeling of love,' he said, 'if you remember its ecstasies, if you ever smiled at the wailing of your new-born son, if ever any human feeling has run through your breast, I entreat you by the feelings of a wife, a lover, a mother, by everything that is sacred in life, not to deny my request! Reveal your secret to me! What is it to you . . ? Perhaps it is bound up with some dreadful sin, with the loss of eternal bliss, with some contract made with the devil . . . Consider: you are old; you have not long to live – I am prepared to take your sins on my own soul. Only reveal to me your secret. Realize that the happiness of a man is in your hands, that not only I, but my children, my grandchildren, my great-grandchildren will bless your memory and will revere it as something sacred . . .'

The old woman answered not a word.

Hermann stood up.

'You old witch!' he said, clenching his teeth. 'I'll force you to answer . . .'

With these words he drew a pistol from his pocket. At the sight of the pistol, the Countess, for the second time, exhibited signs of strong emotion. She shook her

head and raising her hand as though to shield herself from the shot, she rolled over on her back and remained motionless.

'Stop this childish behaviour now,' Hermann said, taking her hand. 'I ask you for the last time: will you name your three cards or won't you?'

The Countess made no reply. Hermann saw that she was dead.

Chapter Four

7 *Mai* 18**
Homme sans mœurs et sans religion!
CORRESPONDENCE

Still in her ball dress, Lisaveta Ivanovna sat in her
room, lost in thought. On her arrival home, she had
quickly dismissed the sleepy maid who had reluctantly
offered her services, had said that she would undress
herself, and with a tremulous heart had gone up to
her room, expecting to find Hermann there and yet
hoping not to find him. Her first glance assured her of
his absence and she thanked her fate for the obstacle
that had prevented their meeting. She sat down, without undressing, and began to recall all the circumstances which had lured her so far in so short a time. It
was not three weeks since she had first seen the young
man from the window – and yet she was already in
correspondence with him, and already he had managed
to persuade her to grant him a nocturnal meeting! She
knew his name only because some of his letters had
been signed; she had never spoken to him, nor heard
his voice, nor heard anything about him . . . until
that very evening. Strange thing! That very evening,
Tomsky, vexed with the Princess Polina *** for not
flirting with him as she usually did, had wished to
revenge himself by a show of indifference: he had
therefore summoned Lisaveta Ivanovna and together
they had danced an endless mazurka. All the time they
were dancing, he had teased her about her partiality to
officers of the Engineers, had assured her that he knew
far more than she would have supposed possible, and
indeed, some of his jests were so successfully aimed that

on several occasions Lisaveta Ivanovna had thought that her secret was known to him.

'From whom have you discovered all this?' she asked, laughing.

'From a friend of the person whom you know so well,' Tomsky answered; 'from a most remarkable man!'

'Who is this remarkable man?'

'He is called Hermann.'

Lisaveta made no reply, but her hands and feet turned quite numb.

'This Hermann,' Tomsky continued, 'is a truly romantic figure: he has the profile of a Napoleon, and the soul of a Mephistopheles. I should think that he has at least three crimes on his conscience. . . . How pale you have turned . . .!'

'I have a headache. . . . What did this Hermann – or whatever his name is – tell you?'

'Hermann is most displeased with his friend: he says that he would act quite differently in his place . . . I even think that Hermann himself has designs on you; at any rate he listens to the exclamations of his enamoured friend with anything but indifference.'

'But where has he seen me?'

'At church, perhaps; on a walk – God only knows! Perhaps in your room, whilst you were asleep: he's quite capable of it . . .'

Three ladies approaching him with the question: 'oublie ou regret?'* interrupted the conversation which had become so agonizingly interesting to Lisaveta Ivanovna.

The lady chosen by Tomsky was the Princess Polina *** herself. She succeeded in clearing up the misunderstanding between them during the many turns

* The words used by a lady in exercising her right, in certain dances, to present herself to her choice of partner on the floor.

and movements of the dance, after which he conducted her to her chair. Tomsky returned to his own place. He no longer had any thoughts for Hermann or Lisaveta Ivanovna, who desperately wanted to renew her interrupted conversation; but the mazurka came to an end and shortly afterwards the old Countess left.

Tomsky's words were nothing but ball-room chatter, but they made a deep impression upon the mind of the young dreamer. The portrait, sketched by Tomsky, resembled the image she herself had formed of Hermann, and thanks to the latest romantic novels, Hermann's quite commonplace face took on attributes that both frightened and captivated her imagination. Now she sat, her uncovered arms crossed, her head, still adorned with flowers, bent over her bare shoulders. . . . Suddenly the door opened, and Hermann entered. She shuddered.

'Where have you been?' she asked in a frightened whisper.

In the old Countess's bedroom,' Hermann answered: 'I have just left it. The Countess is dead.'

'Good God! What are you saying?'

'And it seems,' Hermann continued, 'that I am the cause of her death.'

Lisaveta Ivanovna looked at him, and the words of Tomsky echoed in her mind: 'he has at least three crimes on his conscience'! Hermann sat down beside her on the window sill and told her everything.

Lisaveta Ivanovna listened to him with horror. So those passionate letters, those ardent demands, the whole impertinent and obstinate pursuit – all that was not love! Money – that was what his soul craved for! It was not she who could satisfy his desire and make him happy! The poor ward had been nothing but the unknowing assistant of a brigand, of the murderer of her aged benefactress! . . . She wept bitterly, in an agony of belated repentance. Hermann looked at her in silence; his heart was also tormented; but neither the tears of the poor girl nor the astounding charm of her grief disturbed his hardened soul. He felt no remorse at the thought of the dead old lady. He felt dismay for only one thing: the irretrievable loss of the secret upon which he had relied for enrichment.

'You are a monster!' Lisaveta Ivanovna said at last.

'I did not wish for her death,' Hermann answered. 'My pistol wasn't loaded.'

They were silent.

The day began to break. Lisaveta Ivanovna extinguished the flickering candle. A pale light lit up her room. She wiped her tear-stained eyes and raised them to Hermann: he sat by the window, his arms folded and with a grim frown on his face. In this position he bore an astonishing resemblance to a portrait of Napoleon. Even Lisaveta Ivanovna was struck by the likeness.

'How am I going to get you out of the house?' Lisaveta Ivanovna said at last. 'I had thought of leading you along the secret staircase, but that would mean going past the Countess's bedroom, and I am afraid.'

'Tell me how to find this secret staircase; I'll go on my own.'

Lisaveta Ivanovna stood up, took a key from her chest of drawers, handed it to Hermann, and gave him detailed instructions. Hermann pressed her cold, unresponsive hand, kissed her bowed head and left.

He descended the winding staircase and once more entered the Countess's bedroom. The dead old lady sat as if turned to stone; her face expressed a deep calm. Hermann stopped before her and gazed at her for a long time, as if wishing to assure himself of the dreadful truth; finally, he went into the study, felt for the door behind the silk wall hangings, and, agitated by strange feelings, he began to descend the dark staircase.

'Along this very staircase,' he thought, 'perhaps at this same hour sixty years ago, in an embroidered coat, his hair dressed *à l'oiseau royal*, his three-cornered hat pressed to his heart, there may have crept into this very bedroom a young and happy man now long since turned to dust in his grave – and today the aged heart of his mistress ceased to beat.'

At the bottom of the staircase Hermann found a door, which he opened with the key Lisaveta Ivanovna had given him, and he found himself in a corridor which led into the street.

Chapter Five

*That evening there appeared before me
the figure of the late Baroness von V**.
She was all in white and she said to me:
'How are you, Mr Councillor!'*

SWEDENBORG

Three days after the fateful night, at nine o'clock in the morning, Hermann set out for the *** monastery, where a funeral service for the dead Countess was going to be held. Although unrepentant, he could not altogether silence the voice of conscience, which kept on repeating: 'You are the murderer of the old woman!' Having little true religious belief, he was extremely superstitious. He believed that the dead Countess could exercise a harmful influence on his life, and he had therefore resolved to be present at the funeral, in order to ask her forgiveness.

The church was full. Hermann could scarcely make his way through the crowd of people. The coffin stood on a rich catafalque beneath a velvet canopy. Within it lay the dead woman, her arms folded upon her chest, and dressed in a white satin robe, with a lace cap on her head. Around her stood the members of her household: servants in black coats, with armorial ribbons upon their shoulders and candles in their hands; the relatives – children, grandchildren, great-grandchildren – in deep mourning. Nobody cried; tears would have been *une affectation*. The Countess was so old that her death could have surprised nobody, and her relatives had long considered her as having outlived herself. A young bishop pronounced the funeral sermon. In simple, moving words, he described the

peaceful end of the righteous woman, who for many
years had been in quiet and touching preparation for a
Christian end. 'The angel of death found her,' the
speaker said, 'waiting for the midnight bridegroom,
vigilant in godly meditation.'* The service was completed with sad decorum. The relatives were the first
to take leave of the body. Then the numerous guests
went up to pay final homage to her who had so long
participated in their frivolous amusements. They were
followed by all the members of the Countess's household, the last of whom was an old housekeeper of the
same age as the Countess. She was supported by two
young girls who led her up to the coffin. She had not
the strength to bow down to the ground – and merely
shed a few tears as she kissed the cold hand of her
mistress. After her, Hermann decided to approach the
coffin. He knelt down and for several minutes lay on
the cold floor, which was strewn with fir branches; at
last he got up, as pale as the dead woman herself; he
went up the steps of the catafalque and bent his head
over the body of the Countess. . . . At that very
moment it seemed to him that the dead woman gave
him a mocking glance, and winked at him. Hermann,
hurriedly stepping back, missed his footing, and
crashed on his back against the ground. He was helped
to his feet. At the same moment, Lisaveta Ivanovna
was carried out in a faint to the porch of the church.
These events disturbed the solemnity of the gloomy
ceremony for a few moments. A subdued murmur
rose among the congregation, and a tall, thin chamber-
lain, a near relative of the dead woman, whispered in
the ear of an Englishman standing by him that the
young officer was the Countess's illegitimate son, to
which the Englishman replied coldly: 'Oh?'

For the whole of that day Hermann was exceedingly

* A reference to the parable of the wise and foolish virgins.

troubled. He went to a secluded inn for dinner and, contrary to his usual custom and in the hope of silencing his inward agitation, he drank heavily. But the wine fired his imagination still more. Returning home, he threw himself on to his bed without undressing, and fell into a heavy sleep.

It was already night when he awoke: the moon lit up his room. He glanced at his watch; it was a quarter to three. He found he could not go back to sleep; he sat down on his bed and thought about the funeral of the old Countess.

At that moment somebody in the street glanced in at his window, and immediately went away again. Hermann paid no attention to the incident. A minute or so later, he heard the door into the front room being opened. Hermann imagined that it was his orderly, drunk as usual, returning from some nocturnal outing. But he heard unfamiliar footsteps and the soft shuffling of slippers. The door opened: a woman in a white dress entered. Hermann mistook her for his old wet-nurse and wondered what could have brought her out at that time of the night. But the woman in white glided across the room and suddenly appeared before him – and Hermann recognized the Countess!

'I have come to you against my will,' she said in a firm voice, 'but I have been ordered to fulfil your request. Three, seven, ace, played in that order, will win for you, but only on condition that you play not more than one card in twenty-four hours, and that you never play again for the rest of your life. I'll forgive you my death if you marry my ward, Lisaveta Ivanovna . . .'

With these words, she turned round quietly, walked towards the door and disappeared, her slippers shuffling. Hermann heard the door in the hall bang, and again saw somebody look in at him through the window.

For a long time Hermann could not recollect his
senses. He went out into the next room. His orderly
was lying asleep on the floor; Hermann could scarcely
wake him. The orderly was, as usual, drunk, and it was
impossible to get any sense out of him. The door into
the hall was locked. Hermann returned to his room, lit
a candle, and recorded the details of his vision.

Chapter Six

'Attendez!'
'How dare you say to me: "Attendez"?'
'Your Excellency, I said: "Attendez, sir"!'

Two fixed ideas can no more exist in one mind than, in the physical sense, two bodies can occupy one and the same place. 'Three, seven, ace' soon eclipsed from Hermann's mind the form of the dead old lady. 'Three, seven, ace' never left his thoughts, were constantly on his lips. At the sight of a young girl, he would say: 'How shapely she is! Just like the three of hearts.' When asked the time, he would reply: 'About seven.' Every pot-bellied man he saw reminded him of an ace. 'Three, seven, ace,' assuming all possible shapes, persecuted him in his sleep: the three bloomed before him in the shape of some luxuriant flower, the seven took on the appearance of a Gothic gateway, the ace – of an enormous spider. To the exclusion of all others, one thought alone occupied his mind – making use of the secret which had cost him so much. He began to think of retirement and of travel. He wanted to try his luck in the public gaming-houses of Paris. Chance spared him the trouble.

There was in Moscow a society of rich gamblers, presided over by the celebrated Chekalinsky, a man whose whole life had been spent at the card table, and who had amassed millions long ago, accepting his winnings in the form of promissory notes and paying his losses with ready money. His long experience had earned him the confidence of his companions, and his open house, his famous cook and his friendliness and gaiety had won him great public respect. He arrived in

Petersburg. The younger generation flocked to his house, forgetting balls for cards, and preferring the enticements of faro to the fascinations of courtship. Narumov took Hermann to meet him.

They passed through a succession of magnificent rooms, full of polite and attentive waiters. Several generals and privy councillors were playing whist; young men, sprawled out on brocade divans, were eating ices and smoking their pipes. In the drawing-room, seated at the head of a long table, around which were crowded about twenty players, the host kept bank. He was a most respectable-looking man of about sixty; his head was covered with silvery grey hair, and his full, fresh face expressed good nature; his eyes, enlivened by a perpetual smile, shone brightly. Narumov introduced Hermann to him. Chekalinsky shook his hand warmly, requesting him not to stand on ceremony, and went on dealing.

The game lasted a long time. More than thirty cards lay on the table. Chekalinsky paused after each round in order to give the players time to arrange their cards, wrote down their losses, listened politely to their demands, and more politely still allowed them to retract any stake accidentally left on the table. At last the game finished. Chekalinsky shuffled the cards and prepared to deal again.

'Allow me to place a stake,' Hermann said, stretching out his hand from behind a fat gentleman who was punting there.

Chekalinsky smiled and nodded silently, as a sign of his consent. Narumov laughingly congratulated Hermann on forswearing a longstanding principle and wished him a lucky beginning.

'I've staked,' Hermann said, as he chalked up the amount, which was very considerable, on the back of his card.

'How much is it?' asked the banker, screwing up his eyes. 'Forgive me, but I can't make it out.'

'47,000 roubles,' Hermann replied.

At these words every head in the room turned, and all eyes were fixed on Hermann.

'He's gone out of his mind!' Narumov thought.

'Allow me to observe to you,' Chekalinsky said with his invariable smile, 'that your stake is extremely high: nobody here has ever put more than 275 roubles on any single card.'

'What of it?' retorted Hermann. 'Do you take me or not?'

Chekalinsky, bowing, humbly accepted the stake.

'However, I would like to say,' he said, 'that, being judged worthy of the confidence of my friends, I can only bank against ready money. For my own part, of course, I am sure that your word is enough, but for the sake of the order of the game and of the accounts, I must ask you to place your money on the card.'

Hermann drew a banknote from his pocket and handed it to Chekalinsky who, giving it a cursory glance, put it on Hermann's card.

He began to deal. On the right a nine turned up, on the left a three.

'The three wins,' said Hermann, showing his card.

A murmur arose among the players. Chekalinsky frowned, but instantly the smile returned to his face.

'Do you wish to take the money now?' he asked Hermann.

'If you would be so kind.'

Chekalinsky drew a number of banknotes from his pocket and settled up immediately. Hermann took up his money and left the table. Narumov was too astounded even to think. Hermann drank a glass of lemonade and went home.

The next evening he again appeared at Chekalinsky's.

The host was dealing. Hermann walked up to the table; the players already there immediately gave way to him. Chekalinsky bowed graciously.

Hermann waited for the next deal, took a card and placed on it his 47,000 roubles together with the winnings of the previous evening.

Chekalinsky began to deal. A knave turned up on the right, a seven on the left.

Hermann showed his seven.

There was a general cry of surprise, and Chekalinsky was clearly disconcerted. He counted out 94,000 roubles and handed them to Hermann, who pocketed them coolly and immediately withdrew.

The following evening Hermann again appeared at the table. Everyone was expecting him; the generals and privy councillors abandoned their whist in order to watch such unusual play. The young officers jumped up from their divans; all the waiters gathered in the drawing-room. Hermann was surrounded by a crowd of people. The other players held back their cards, impatient to see how Hermann would get on. Hermann stood at the table and prepared to play alone against the pale but still smiling Chekalinsky. Each unsealed a pack of cards. Chekalinsky shuffled. Hermann drew and placed his card, covering it with a heap of banknotes. It was like a duel. A deep silence reigned all around.

His hands shaking, Chekalinsky began to deal. On the right lay a queen, on the left an ace.

'The ace wins,' said Hermann and showed his card.

'Your queen has lost,' Chekalinsky said kindly.

Hermann started: indeed, instead of an ace, before him lay the queen of spades. He could not believe his eyes, could not understand how he could have slipped up.

At that moment it seemed to him that the queen of

spades winked at him and smiled. He was struck by an unusual likeness . . .

'The old woman!' he shouted in terror.

Chekalinsky gathered up his winnings. Hermann stood motionless. When he left the table, people began to converse noisily.

'Famously punted!' the players said.

Chekalinsky shuffled the cards afresh; play went on as usual.

CONCLUSION

Hermann went mad. He is now installed in Room 17 at the Obukhov Hospital; he answers no questions, but merely mutters with unusual rapidity: 'Three, seven, ace! Three, seven, queen!'

Lisaveta Ivanovna has married a very agreeable young man, who has a good position in the service somewhere; he is the son of the former steward of the old Countess. Lisaveta Ivanovna is bringing up a poor relative.

Tomsky has been promoted to the rank of Captain, and is going to marry Princess Polina.

1833

The Captain's Daughter

Look after your honour when it is young.

SAYING

1. A Sergeant of the Guards

— He could enter the Guards as a captain tomorrow.
— But there's no need for that; let him serve in the ranks.
— Well spoken! Let him learn the hard way . . . .
And who is his father?

KNYAZHNIN: *The Braggart*

My father, Andrei Petrovitch Grinev, served under Count Münnich* in his youth and retired from the service in the year 17** as a lieutenant-colonel. He then went to live on his estate in the district of Simbirsk,† where he married Avdotya Vassilyevna U**, the daughter of a poor local nobleman. There were nine of us children. All my brothers and sisters died in their infancy. Thanks to Prince B**, a major in the Guards and a close relative of the family, I was registered as a sergeant in the Semyonovsky regiment. If, contrary to all expectations, my mother had given birth to a daughter, my father would have informed the appropriate quarters of the death of the sergeant who had failed to appear, and there the matter would have ended. I was considered to be on leave of absence until the completion of my studies. Children were not brought up in those days as they are today. At the age of five, I was entrusted to the care of our senior groom, Savyelitch, whose sober conduct had rendered him worthy of being my personal attendant. By the age of

---

* 1683–1767; field-marshal and politician who served under Peter the Great, but who was exiled to Siberia in 1741.
† Now Ulyanov: town on the Volga some 450 miles east of Moscow.

twelve, under his supervision, I had learned to read and write Russian and I was a sound judge of the qualities of a greyhound. At this time my father engaged for me a Frenchman, a Monsieur Beaupré, who had been sent for from Moscow together with the yearly supply of wine and olive oil. His arrival greatly displeased Savyelitch.

'Heaven be thanked,' he used to grumble to himself, 'that the child is apparently washed, combed and well-fed. Why waste money getting a "Monsoo"? – as if we hadn't enough of our own people here!'

In his own country, Beaupré had been a hairdresser, then a soldier in Prussia, and then he had come to Russia *pour être outchitel* without a very clear idea of the meaning of the word. He was a good-natured fellow, but flighty and extremely dissolute. His chief weakness was a passion for the fair sex; his tender advances were not infrequently met with slaps, which caused him to groan for hours and hours on end. Furthermore, he was (to use his expression) 'no enemy of the bottle', which (in Russian) means that he liked a drop too much. But since, with us, wine was only served at dinner, and then only one glass each, and since the tutor's glass was generally passed over, my Beaupré very soon became accustomed to home-made Russian brews and even began to prefer them to the wines of his own country, claiming that they were far better for the stomach. We made friends immediately, and although the contract obliged him to teach me French, German and all the sciences, he was quick to show that he preferred to learn some scraps of Russian from me – after which we each did as we wished. Our relationship was one of the utmost harmony. I wished for no other mentor. But fate soon parted us, and here is how:

It so happened that one day the laundress, Palashka, a fat, pock-marked wench and the one-eyed dairymaid, Akulka, decided jointly to throw themselves at my mother's feet and, confessing to a criminal weakness, tearfully complained that 'Monsoo' had taken advantage of their inexperience. My mother did not treat such affairs lightly and conferred with my father on the subject. With him, justice was swiftly executed. He instantly sent for that rogue, the Frenchman. He was informed that 'Monsoo' was giving me my lesson. My father went up to my room.

At that moment Beaupré was on the bed, sleeping the sleep of the innocent. I was amusing myself in my own way. I should say that a geographical map had been sent from Moscow for me. It used to hang on the wall, where it was put to no use whatever, and I had long been tempted by the size and quality of its paper. I decided to use it for my own purposes, and taking advantage of the sleeping Beaupré, I set to work. My father came in at the very moment I was fitting a bast tail to the Cape of Good Hope. Seeing the extent of my geographical exercises, my father boxed me round the ear, and then hastening over to Beaupré, he roused him in extremely brusque fashion and began to heap reproaches on him. In his confusion Beaupré attempted to stand up but could not: the unfortunate Frenchman was dead drunk. As well be hanged for a sheep as for a lamb. My father lifted him off the bed by his collar, pushed him out of the door and banished him from the premises that very same day, to the indescribable joy of Savyelitch. Thus ended my education.

I now lived a life of youthful leisure, chasing pigeons and playing leap-frog with the other boys on the estate. In the meantime, I had turned sixteen. At this point, my fate underwent a change.

One autumn day, my mother was making some honey-jam in the parlour while I, licking my lips, looked at the boiling scum. My father was sitting at the window, reading the 'Court Calendar' which he received every year. This book always had a powerful effect on him: he used to read it with particular interest, and his reading of it always stirred his bile in the most remarkable fashion. My mother, who had a sure knowledge of all his ways and habits, always endeavoured to shove the wretched book as far out of sight as possible, and in this way the 'Court Calendar' would sometimes evade his eyes for whole months at a time. But when my father did happen to find it, he would not let it out of his hands for hours on end. Thus, my father was reading the 'Court Calendar', from time to time shrugging his shoulders and muttering:

'Lieutenant-general . . . ! He was a sergeant in my company . . . ! Knight of both Russian orders . . . ! How long ago was it that we . . . ?'

At length my father flung the 'Calendar' down on the sofa and sank into a reverie, a habit of his which boded nothing but ill.

Suddenly he turned to my mother.

'Avdotya Vassilyevna, how old is Petrusha?'

'He's nearly seventeen,' replied my mother. 'Petrusha was born the same year that aunt Nastasya Gerassimovna lost her eye, and when . . .'

'Very well,' interrupted my father. 'It's time he entered the Service. He's had enough of running about the maids' workrooms and climbing the dovecotes.'

The thought that she should soon be parted from me had such an effect upon my mother that she dropped the spoon into the saucepan, and the tears poured down her face. My own delight, on the other hand, could scarcely be described. The thought of the Service was connected in my mind with thoughts of freedom and the pleasures of life in Petersburg. I pictured myself as an officer of the Guards – in my opinion, the summit of worldly happiness.

My father liked neither to alter his intentions nor to delay their execution. A day was appointed for my departure. On the evening before, my father announced that he proposed to send a letter by me to my future commanding officer and he demanded pen and paper.

'Don't forget, Andrei Petrovitch,' my mother said, 'to send my best wishes to Prince B**, and say that I hope he'll treat Petrusha kindly.'

'What nonsense is this!' my father replied, frowning. 'Why should I be writing to Prince B**?'

'But you said a moment ago that you were going to write to Petrusha's commanding officer.'

'Well, and so what?'

'But Petrusha's commanding officer is Prince B**. Petrusha's registered with the Semyonovsky regiment.'

'Registered! What do I care whether he's registered? Petrusha's not going to Petersburg. What would he learn by serving in Petersburg? To squander his money and behave like a rake. No, let him serve in the real army; let him learn to toil and drudge, to smell powder; let him be a soldier and not a mere idler. Registered with the Guards! Where's his passport? Bring it here.'

My mother got out my passport, which she kept in her little box together with my christening robe, and gave it to my father with a trembling hand. My father read it through carefully, put it on the table before him and began his letter.

I was tormented by curiosity. Where was I to be sent, if not to Petersburg? I could not tear my eyes away from my father's pen which moved slowly enough over the paper. At last he finished, sealed the letter in the same packet as my passport, removed his spectacles, and calling me to him, said:

'Here is a letter for Andrei Karlovitch R**, an old

friend and comrade of mine. You're going to Orenburg * to serve under his command.'

And so all my brilliant hopes were shattered! Instead of a gay life in Petersburg, boredom awaited me
in some dreary and distant part of the country. The
Service, which, until a moment before, I had thought
of with such rapture, now struck me as a grievous misfortune. But it was useless to argue.

On the morning of the following day a travelling-
carriage was brought round to the steps; in it were
packed my trunk and a hamper containing a tea-
service and parcels of buns and pies – final tokens of
home indulgence. My parents gave me their blessing.
My father said to me:

'Good-bye, Pyotr. Serve faithfully whom you have
sworn to serve: obey your superiors, do not seek their
favours; don't thrust yourself forward for service, but
don't shirk your duty; and remember the proverb:
"Look after your clothes when they're new and your
honour when it's young." '

My mother tearfully besought me to take care of my
health, and Savyelitch to watch over his charge. They
helped me on with my hareskin coat and, over that,
another one of fox fur. I sat down in the carriage with
Savyelitch and set off on my journey, the tears
streaming down my face.

That same night I arrived at Simbirsk where I was
to spend the whole of the next day so that Savyelitch,
who had been entrusted with the task, could buy
several articles I needed. I stayed at an inn. In the
morning, Savyelitch set off for the shops. Tired of
looking out of the window on to a dirty alley-way, I
began to wander about the other rooms of the inn.
Entering the billiards-room, I saw a tall gentleman of

* Town in the southern Urals some 320 miles south-east of Simbirsk.

about thirty-five with a long black moustache; he was
in his dressing-gown and had a cue in one hand and a
pipe between his teeth. He was playing with the
marker, who drank down a glass of vodka every time
he won, but who, when he lost, was obliged to crawl
on all fours under the billiards-table. I stopped to watch
them play. The longer the game went on, the more
frequently did the marker have to crawl about on all
fours, until eventually he remained beneath the table.
The gentleman uttered several forceful expressions
over him as a sort of funeral oration and invited me to
have a game with him. Not knowing how to play, I
refused. This seemed to strike him as strange. He
looked at me as if with commiseration. However, we
got into conversation and I learned that he was called
Ivan Ivanovitch Zurin, that he was a captain in the
*** Hussar regiment, that he was in Simbirsk for the
reception of some recruits, and that he was staying at
the inn.

Zurin invited me to take pot-luck and dine with him
in military fashion. I readily accepted his invitation.
We sat down at table. Zurin drank a great deal and
urged me to do the same, saying that I must become
accustomed to the ways of the Service; he related
several military anecdotes which nearly made me die
of laughter, and we got up from the table firm friends.
He then offered to teach me to play billiards.

'It's essential that we soldiers should know how to
play. On the march, for instance, you arrive at some
small town. How are you going to amuse yourself?
One can't always be beating up the Jews. And so, for
want of something better, you go to the inn and start to
play billiards; to do that you must know how to play!'

I was completely convinced and set about learning
the game with great diligence. Zurin loudly encouraged me, showed surprise at my rapid progress and

after a few lessons proposed that we should play for
money – only a small stake and not for the sake of gain,
but merely that we should not play for nothing, which
he held to be a most odious practice. I agreed with him,
and Zurin ordered me some punch which he persuaded me to try, repeating that I must get used to the
life in the Service; what kind of a Service would it be
without punch! I obeyed him. All the while we continued our game. The more frequently I sipped from
my glass, the more daring did I become. The balls
kept flying over the cushion; I became heated, abused
the marker, who was keeping the score heaven only
knows how, increased the stake from time to time – in
short behaved like a boy with his first taste of freedom.
Time slipped imperceptibly by, Zurin glanced at his
watch, put down his cue, and announced that I had
lost one hundred roubles. I was somewhat confused
by this declaration. Savyelitch had my money. I began
to apologize. Zurin interrupted me:

'Pray, don't bother yourself worrying. I can wait,
and meanwhile let's go to Arinushka's.'

What would you have me do? I finished the day as
dissolutely as I had begun it. We had supper at Arinushka's. Zurin kept filling my glass, repeating that I
must get used to the ways of the Service. When I rose
from the table, I could scarcely stand up straight. At
midnight Zurin drove me back to the inn.

Savyelitch met us on the steps. He groaned as he saw
the unmistakable signs of my enthusiasm for the Service.

'What's happened to you, master?' he said in a
sorrowful voice. 'Where did you get so loaded like that?
Oh Lord, never before have you done such a dreadful
thing!'

'Silence, you old grumbler!' I replied in an unsteady
voice. 'You must be drunk. Go to sleep . . . and put me
to bed.'

I woke the next morning with a splitting headache and a hazy recollection of the events of the previous evening. My reflections were interrupted by Savyelitch who entered my room with a cup of tea.

'You've started early on your pranks, Pyotr Andreitch,' he said, shaking his head. 'And who is it that you take after? It's certain that neither your father nor grandfather were drunkards. It goes without saying that your mother isn't – since the day of her birth she has never touched anything but kvass. Who is to blame for all this? That accursed "Monsoo". He was perpetually running round to Antipyevna's with *"Madame, zhe voo pree, vodkyoo"*. Well there's *zhe voo pree* for you! It can't be denied, that son of a bitch taught you some pretty habits! And that infidel tutor had to be engaged for you – as if the master hadn't enough of his own people!'

I was ashamed. I turned away from him and said:

'Go away, Savyelitch; I don't want any tea.'

But it was a difficult matter to quieten Savyelitch when he was bent on delivering a sermon.

'Now you can see, Pyotr Andreitch, what it is to get drunk. You've got a bad head and don't want to eat anything. A man who drinks is fit for nothing. Drink up some cucumber pickle with honey, or best of all for the morning after, half a glass of home-made brandy. What do you say?'

At that moment a boy entered the room and handed me a note from Ivan Ivanovitch Zurin. I opened it and read the following

Dear Pyotr Andreyevitch,
Be so good as to send me, by the boy, the hundred roubles you lost to me yesterday. I am in urgent need of money.
Always at your service,
Ivan Zurin.

There was nothing for it. I assumed an air of indifference and turning to Savyelitch, who was my treasurer, housekeeper and agent all in one, I ordered him to give the boy one hundred roubles.

'What? Why? What for!' asked the astonished Savyelitch.

'I owe them to him,' I replied as coolly as I could.

'Owe!' exclaimed Savyelitch, becoming more and more astonished. 'And when, master, did you find time to get into his debt? I don't like the sound of this. You may do as you please, master, but I'm not going to give you the money.'

I thought that if, at this decisive moment, I did not gain the upper hand of the obstinate old man, it would be difficult to free myself from his tutelage later on, and so, looking at him haughtily, I said:

'I am your master and you are my servant. It is my money. I lost it gambling because I took it into my head to do so. I advise you not to philosophize about it and do as you are told.'

Savyelitch was so struck by my words that he clasped his hands and stood as if turned to stone.

'What are you standing there like that for?' I shouted angrily.

Savyelitch began to weep.

'Pyotr Andreitch, my dear,' he said in a trembling voice, 'do not cause me to die of a broken heart. Light of my life, listen to me, an old man! Write to that brigand and say that you were joking, that we are not in the habit even of having that much money. One hundred roubles! God be merciful! Tell him that your parents expressly forbade you to gamble with anything but nuts . . .'

'That's enough!' I interrupted him severely. 'Hand over the money or I'll throw you out by the scruff of your neck.'

Savyelitch looked at me with the deepest grief and
went to fetch my debt. I felt sorry for the poor old man,
but I wanted to assert my independence and show him
that I was no longer a child. The money was delivered
to Zurin. Savyelitch made haste to take me away from
the accursed inn. He came to me with the news that
the horses were ready. With an uneasy conscience and
filled with silent remorse, I left Simbirsk, without
saying good-bye to my billiards-teacher and without
thinking that I should ever see him again.

2. The Guide

O land of mine,
Unfamiliar land!
It is not I who wished to go to you,
It is not my good horse which took me,
But youth and liveliness,
A young man's spirit,
And tavern wine.

AN OLD SONG

My reflections during the journey were not particularly agreeable. My loss, in terms of the value of money at that time, was of no small importance. In my heart, I could not but confess that my behaviour at the inn in Simbirsk had been foolish, and I felt guilty before Savyelitch. All this distressed me. The old man sat sullenly on the box, his face turned away from me and but for an occasional sigh he was silent. I wanted at all costs to make it up with him but I did not know how to begin. Finally, I said to him:

'Come now, Savyelitch! That's enough, let us be friends; it was all my fault; I can see myself that I was wrong. I behaved extremely foolishly yesterday and offended you for no reason. I promise that I'll conduct myself more sensibly in future and listen to you. Now don't be angry; let us make our peace.'

'Ah, Pyotr Andreitch, my dear,' he answered with a deep sigh. 'I'm angry with myself; it is I alone who am to blame. How could I have left you alone in the inn! But what could I do? I was tempted by the devil: I took it into my head to drop in on the clerk's wife who is an old friend of mine. And there it is: I drop in on an old friend, and see what happens. A real calamity! How shall I ever be able to show myself before my master and mistress again? What will they say when they learn that their child is a drunkard and a gambler?'

In order to console poor Savyelitch, I gave him my word that in future I would not spend a single copeck without his consent. He gradually calmed down; although from time to time, shaking his head, he still muttered to himself:

'One hundred roubles! It's no joke!'

I was drawing near to my destination. All around me stretched a desolate wilderness, intersected by hills and ravines. Everything was covered with snow. The sun was setting. The sledge was travelling along the narrow road, or, to be more precise, along the track made by the sledges of the peasants. Suddenly the driver began to look around him and eventually, taking off his cap, he turned to me and said:

'Won't you order me to turn back, sir?'

'Why?'

'The weather doesn't look too hopeful: the wind is beginning to rise. See how it's heaping up the newly-fallen snow.'

'There's no great harm in that.'

'And do you see over there?'

The driver pointed eastwards with his whip.

'I see nothing but white steppe and a clear sky.'

'But there – over there – that small cloud.'

Indeed, on the edge of the horizon, I saw a small white cloud, which at first I had wrongly taken for a distant hill. The driver explained to me that the little cloud presaged a snow-storm.

I had heard about the snow-storms in that part of the country, and knew that whole wagon-trains were sometimes buried by them. Savyelitch agreed with the driver and advised that we should turn back. But the wind did not strike me as being especially strong. I was hoping to be able the reach the next posting-station in good time, and ordered the driver to go on faster.

The driver set the horses at a gallop, but he still continued to look eastwards. The horses ran on harmoniously. The wind, meanwhile, was growing stronger every minute. The little cloud changed into a great white mass, which rose heavily, grew, and gradually began to spread across the whole sky. At first a fine snow – and then, suddenly, big snowflakes – began to fall. The wind howled; the storm burst upon us. In a moment the dark sky merged with the sea of snow; everything vanished.

'Well, sir,' cried the driver. 'We are in for it – a blizzard!'

I looked out of the sledge: all was darkness and whirlwind. The wind howled with such ferocious violence that it seemed as though it were alive; Savyelitch and I became covered with snow. The horses slowed down to a walking pace and soon stopped altogether.

'Why don't you go on?' I asked the driver impatiently.

'What's the use?' he asked, jumping down from the box. God knows where we're going as it is; there's no road and all around is darkness.'

I began to scold him. Savyelitch took his part.

'Why didn't you want to listen to him?' he said angrily. 'You should have returned to the posting-station, where you could have had some tea and slept undisturbed until morning, when the storm would have abated and we could have gone on. Anyway, what's the hurry? It would be all very well if we were going to a wedding!'

Savyelitch was right. There was nothing we could do. The snow was falling hard. A snowdrift was piling up around the sledge. The horses stood with bent heads, and from time to time a shudder would run

through their bodies. Having nothing else to do, the
driver kept walking round them, arranging the harness. Savyelitch grumbled; I looked everywhere
around me in the hope of catching sight of some sign
of a house or a road, but could distinguish nothing save
the dense, whirling snow-storm . . . Suddenly I saw
something black.

'Hey, driver!' I shouted. 'Look! What's that black
thing over there?'

The driver began to peer in the direction I was
pointing.

'Heaven knows, sir,' he said, sitting down in his
seat again. 'It's certainly not a cart or a tree, and it
seems to be moving. It must be a wolf or a man.'

I ordered him to drive towards the unknown object,
which immediately started to move towards us. A
couple of minutes later we had drawn level with the
man.

'Hey, my good man!' the driver shouted to him. 'Do
you know where the road is?'

'The road's here; I am standing on a firm strip,' the
wayfarer replied, 'but what's the good in that?'

'Listen here, my man,' I said to him, 'do you know
this part of the country? Can you take me to a night's
lodgings?'

'I know the country well,' the wayfarer replied.
'Heaven be thanked, I have tramped and driven over it
in every direction. But you can see what the weather's
like: we would be sure to lose the way. You'd better
stop here and wait – perhaps the storm will abate and
the sky clear; then we can find our way by the stars.'

His composure encouraged me. I had already
resolved to commit myself into the hands of God and
spend the night in the middle of the steppe, when
suddenly the wayfarer climbed nimbly up on to the
box and said to the driver:

'Heaven be thanked, there's a house near by; turn to the right and then go straight on.'

'But why should I turn to the right?' the driver asked with irritation. 'Where do you see the road? I know, I know, the horses don't belong to you and neither does the harness, so drive on, eh, drive on.'

The driver seemed to me to be right.

'Indeed,' I said, 'what makes you think that we're not far from a house?'

'Because the wind came from that direction,' the traveller replied, 'and I smelt smoke. That shows that there's a village near by.'

His resourcefulness and keen sense of smell astonished me. I ordered the driver to go on. The horses stepped heavily through the thick snow. The sledge advanced slowly, now mounting a snowdrift, now sinking into a hollow, at one moment rolling to one side, at the next to the other. It was like being aboard a ship in a stormy sea. Savyelitch groaned as he continually jostled against my side. I let down the matting which served as a hood to the sledge, wrapped myself up in my cloak and dozed off, lulled by the song of the storm and by the rocking of our slow journey.

I had a dream which I have never been able to forget, and in which, to this day, I still see something prophetic when I compare it with the strange events of my life. The reader will forgive me for mentioning it since he probably knows from experience that man is naturally given to superstition, however great is his contempt for such prejudices.

I was in that condition of mind and feeling when reality gives way to dreaming and becomes merged into the hazy visions of the first stages of sleep. It seemed to me that the storm was still raging, and that we were still roaming about in the wilderness of snow . . . Suddenly I saw a gateway and drove into the courtyard of our estate. My first thought was one of fear that my father would be angry with me for my involuntary return to the paternal roof, and that he would look upon it as a deliberate act of disobedience. With a feeling of uneasiness I jumped down from the sledge and saw my mother coming down the steps to meet me, a look of deep grief upon her face.

'Quietly,' she says to me. 'Your father is ill and dying and wishes to take leave of you.'

Struck with fear, I follow her into the bedroom. I see that the room is weakly lit and that a collection of sad-faced people stand by the bed. I approach the bed softly; my mother raises the curtain and says:

'Andrei Petrovitch, Petrusha has arrived; he came back when he heard that you were ill; give him your blessing.'

I went down on my knees and fixed my eyes on the sick man. But what's happened? . . . I see, in place of my father, a black-bearded peasant gaily looking at me.

Perplexed, I turned to my mother and said:

'What does this mean? This isn't my father. Why must I ask this peasant for his blessing?'

'It's all the same, Petrusha,' my mother answered me. 'This is your father by proxy; kiss his hand and allow him to give you his blessing.'

I did not consent to this. Then the peasant leaped out of bed, seized an axe from behind his back and began to swing it about in every direction. I wanted to run . . . but I could not. The room was full of dead bodies; I kept stumbling against them and slipping in the pools of blood. . . . The terrible peasant called to me gently and said:

'Don't be frightened. Come and receive my blessing.'

Horror and perplexity took hold of me . . . At that moment I awoke; the horses had stopped; Savyelitch was holding my arm and saying:

'Get out, master, come on. We've arrived.'

'Where have we arrived?' I asked, rubbing my eyes.

'At a country inn. The Lord came to our aid, and we bumped straight into the fence. Quickly, master, come and warm yourself.'

I got out of the sledge. The storm still continued, although with less violence. It was pitch dark. The innkeeper met us at the gate, holding a lantern under the skirt of his overcoat, and led me into a room which was small but reasonably clean; it was lit by a pine torch. On the wall hung a rifle and a tall Cossack cap.

The innkeeper, a Yaikian Cossack* by birth, seemed to be a peasant of about sixty, still quite hale and fresh-faced. Savyelitch followed me in with the hamper and demanded a fire so that he could make some tea, which had never before seemed so necessary to me. The innkeeper went out to see to this.

'Where is the guide?' I asked Savyelitch.

'Here, your Honour,' replied a voice from above.

I looked up at the sleeping shelf above the stove and saw a black beard and two sparkling eyes.

'Well, friend, are you thoroughly frozen?'

'How otherwise in a single thin overcoat! But I'll be frank with you – I did have a sheepskin coat, but I pawned it yesterday with a publican; the frost did not seem to me to be so sharp.'

At that moment the innkeeper came in with a boiling samovar; I offered our guide a cup of tea; the peasant climbed down from the shelf. His appearance struck me as remarkable. He was about forty, of medium height, lean and broad-shouldered. His black beard was beginning to go grey: his large lively eyes

* Cossack from the region of the Yaik river, renamed Ural river after the Pugachev uprisings. The Yaikian Cossacks constituted a separate military organization, but after their revolt in 1772 all their military privileges were annulled.

were for ever darting about. His face had quite an
agreeable but roguish expression to it. His hair had
been cropped in a circle round his head; he wore a
tattered overcoat and Tartar trousers. I handed him a
cup of tea; he tasted it and pulled a face.

'Your Honour, be so good as to tell them to bring me
a glass of wine; tea is not the drink for us Cossacks.'

I readily fulfilled his wish. The innkeeper took a
square bottle and a glass from the cupboard, went up to
him, and looking him in the face, said:

'Oh, so you're back in this area again! Where have
you come from?'

My guide winked significantly and replied with this
saying:

'I was flying about the kitchen-garden, pecking
hempseed; the old woman threw a stone at me but it
missed. And what about your people?'

'Oh, our people!' replied the innkeeper, continuing
the allegorical conversation. 'They were about to ring
the bells for vespers, but the priest's wife refused to
allow it: when the priest is out visiting, the devils play
pranks in the graveyard.'

'Silence, uncle,' replied my vagabond. 'If it rains,
there'll be mushrooms, and when there are mushrooms, there's a bark basket too. But now' – and here
he winked again – 'hide your axe behind your back:
the forester's about. Your Honour – your health!'

With these words he took his glass, crossed himself
and drank down the contents in a single gulp. He then
bowed to me and returned to his shelf.

I could not understand a single word of this thieves'
slang at the time; but afterwards I guesssed that it
referred to the affairs of the Yaikian Army who had
only just been brought to order after the revolt of
1772. Savyelitch listened with an air of profound displeasure. He kept looking suspiciously now at the

innkeeper, now at the guide. The inn or 'umet' * as it was called locally, lay on its own in the middle of the steppe, far from any village, and looked very much as though it were a thieves' meeting-place. But there was no help for it. It was impossible to think of continuing our journey. Savyelitch's anxiety gave me great amusement. Meanwhile, I made arrangements for the night and lay down on the bench. Savyelitch decided to make a place for himself on the stove; the innkeeper lay down on the floor. Soon the whole hut was snoring and I fell into a deep sleep.

Waking rather late the following morning, I saw that the storm had abated. The sun was shining. The snow lay like a dazzling shroud over the boundless steppe. The horses were harnessed. I settled my account with the innkeeper, who charged us such a moderate sum that even Savyelitch made no attempt to quarrel and bargain with him as he usually did, and his suspicions of the previous evening vanished entirely from his head. I called the guide, thanked him for the help he had given us, and ordered Savyelitch to tip him half a rouble. Savyelitch frowned.

'Tip him half a rouble!' he said. 'What for? Because you were pleased to bring him with you to the inn. Do as you wish, master, but we haven't any half-roubles to spare. If we start handing round tips to everyone we meet, we'll soon have to starve ourselves.'

I could not argue with Savyelitch. I had promised that he should be completely in charge of the money. I felt vexed, however, at not being able to reward the man who had rescued me, if not from utter disaster, at least from a very unpleasant situation.

'All right,' I said coldly, 'if you don't want to give him half a rouble, then give him something of mine to wear. He is too lightly dressed. Give him my hareskin coat.'

* A military term for shelter or trench.

'Mercy on us, dear Pyotr Andreitch!' Savyelitch said. 'Why give him your hareskin coat? The dog will only sell it for a drink at the first pub he gets to.'

'It's none of your business, old man,' my vagabond said, 'whether I sell it or not. His Honour wishes to give me a coat from off his own shoulders: it is the will of your master, and your duty as a serf is not to argue but to obey.'

'Have you no fear of God, you brigand?' Savyelitch answered him in an angry voice. 'You can see that the child is still completely ignorant, and yet you are only too glad to take advantage of his innocence. Why do you want my master's coat? You'll not be able to fit it across your accursed shoulders.'

'Will you please be quiet,' I said, 'and bring the coat here immediately.'

'Good Lord above!' Savyelitch groaned. 'Your hareskin coat is almost brand-new! Give it to someone who deserves it, not to a bare-faced drunkard!'

However, the hareskin coat appeared. The peasant instantly began to try it on. Indeed, the coat, which even I had outgrown, was a little too tight on him. Nevertheless, he managed to struggle into it somehow, bursting the seams as he did so. Savyelitch nearly howled as he heard the stitches give way. The vagabond was extremely pleased with my present. He went with me to the sledge and said with a low bow:

'Thank you, your Honour! May the Lord reward you for your kindness. As long as I live, I shall never forget your goodness.'

He went on his own way and I again set out on mine, paying no attention to Savyelitch's vexed condition, and I soon forgot about the snow-storm of the previous day, about my guide and the hareskin coat.

On arriving at Orenburg, I immediately presented myself to the general. I saw a tall man, already

somewhat bent with age. His long hair was completely
white. His old and faded uniform recalled a soldier of
the time of the Empress Anna Ioannovna,* and he
spoke with a strong German accent. I handed him my
father's letter. At his name, he glanced at me quickly.

'*Mein Gott!*' he said. 'It doesn't seem long ago that
Andrei Petrovitch was himself your age; and now
what a fine young son he's got for himself! *Ach*, how
time flies!'

He unsealed the letter and began to read it in a low
voice, making his own observations as he did so.

' "Esteemed Sir, Andrei Karlovitch, I hope that your
Excellency . . ." Why so formal? Pshaw, he should
be ashamed of himself! Of course, discipline before
everything, but is that the way to write to an old comrade? . . . "Your Excellency will not have forgotten
. . ." Hm . . . "And when the late Field-Marshal
Münnich . . . in the campaign . . . little Caroline
also . . ." *Ach, Bruder!* So he still remembers our old
pranks? "Now to business . . . I'm sending my young
rascal to you . . ." Hm . . . "Handle him with
hedgehog gloves . . ." What are hedgehog gloves?
It must be a Russian saying . . . What does "handle
him with hedgehog gloves" mean?' he repeated,
turning to me.

'It means,' I replied, looking as innocent as I possibly
could, 'to treat someone kindly, not to be too severe, to
allow as much freedom as possible – that's "to handle
with hedgehog gloves".'

'Hm, I understand . . . "and do not allow him too
much freedom . . ." No, it's clear that "to handle
with hedgehog gloves" doesn't mean that . . . "En-
closed . . . his passport . . ." Where is it, though?
Ah here we are . . . "Strike him off the register of

* Niece of Peter the Great, widowed Duchess of Courland, reigned
1730–40.

the Semyonovsky regiment . . ." All right, all right:
everything shall be done . . . "Permit me to embrace
you without ceremony and . . . as an old friend and
comrade . . ." Ah, at last he's come to it! . . . etc.,
etc. . . . Well, my boy,' he said when he had finished
reading the letter and had put my passport to one side,
'everything shall be attended to: you will be transferred as an officer into the *** regiment, and, so as
not to lose time, you will leave tomorrow for the
Belogorsky fortress, where you will be under the command of Captain Mironov, a good and honourable
man. There you will see some real service and be
taught the meaning of discipline. There's nothing for
you to do here in Orenburg. Dissipation is harmful to
a young man. Do me the favour of dining with me this
evening.'

'It's getting worse and worse,' I thought to myself.
'What's the use of having been a sergeant in the
Guards almost since the time I was in my mother's
womb! Where has it lead me? To the *** regiment,
and to an out-of-the-way fortress on the borders of the
Kirghiz-Kaissak steppes!' *

I dined with Andrei Karlovitch, in company with his
aged adjutant. A strict German economy governed the
table, and I believe that the fear of an additional guest
now and then at his bachelor's table was in part the
cause of my speedy banishment to the garrison.

The next day I took my leave of the general and set
out for my destination.

* Region east of the river Ural, now territory of the Kazakh SSR.

3. The Fortress

In this fortress we live,
Bread we eat and water we drink,
But when the fierce enemy
Comes to try out our pies,
A great feast we will prepare for our
*   guests,*
And our cannon we will load with grape-
*   shot.*   SOLDIER'S SONG

They are old-fashioned people, dear sir.
    FONVIZIN: *The Minor*

The Belogorsky fortress was situated forty versts from
Orenburg. The road ran along the steep bank of the
Yaik. The river was not yet frozen and its leaden-
coloured waves looked black and melancholy between
the monotonous, snow-covered banks. Beyond it
stretched the Kirghiz steppes. I was deep in reflection,
for the most part of a gloomy nature. Garrison life
held little attraction for me. I tried to picture Captain
Mironov, my future commanding officer, and the
picture that came to my mind was that of a strict,
bad-tempered old man, knowing nothing outside the
Service, and ready to put me under arrest on bread and
water for the merest trifle. Meanwhile, it was beginning to grow dark. We were driving pretty fast.

'Is it far to the fortress?' I asked my driver.

'Not far,' he replied. 'You can see it over there.'

I looked around me in every direction, expecting to
see menacing bastions, towers and a rampart; but all I
could see was a little village surrounded by a thick
wooden fence. On one side of it stood three or four haystacks, half-concealed beneath the snow; on the other, a
dilapidated windmill with idly-hanging bark sails.

'But where is the fortress?' I asked in surprise.

'There it is,' replied the driver, indicating the little village, and as he spoke, we drove into it.

At the gates I saw an old cast-iron cannon; the streets were narrow and twisting; the cottages small and for the most part thatched. I ordered the driver to take me to the commandant, and a minute later, the sledge stopped before a small wooden house, built on a rise in the ground near the church, which was also made of wood.

Nobody came out to meet me. I went up to the entrance and opened a door into the front hall. An old soldier, seated on a table, was sewing a blue patch on the elbow of a green uniform. I told him to announce me.

'Go in, my good chap,' the old soldier replied. 'Our people are at home.'

I entered a neat, clean room, furnished in the old-fashioned style. In one corner stood a china cupboard; attached to the wall was an officer's diploma, glazed and framed; in bright array around it hung cheap, coloured prints representing 'The Taking of Küstrin', * 'The Taking of Ochakov',† 'The Choice of a Bride' and 'The Cat's Funeral'. An old woman wearing a warm sleeveless jacket and with a handkerchief over her head was sitting at the window. She was unwinding some thread which a one-eyed old man in officer's uniform was holding outstretched in his hands.

'What can I do for you, good sir?' she asked, continuing with her work.

I replied that I had come to enter the Service and to present myself to the captain in accordance with my duty, and with these words, I turned to the one-eyed

* A Prussian fortress taken in 1758 by the Russians during the Seven Years' War.
† Turkish fortress taken by the Russians in 1737.

old man, whom I took to be the commandant; the lady of the house, however, interrupted the speech that I had prepared.

'Ivan Kuzmitch is not at home,' she said. 'He has gone to visit Father Gerassim; but it's all the same, dear sir, for I am his wife. I hope that we shall become friends. Please sit down.'

She summoned the maid and ordered her to call for the sergeant. The old man looked at me curiously with his one eye.

'May I venture to ask,' he said, 'in which regiment you have been serving?'

I satisfied his curiosity.

'And may I ask,' he continued, 'why you have transferred from the Guards to this garrison?'

I replied that such was the wish of the authorities.

'For conduct unbecoming an officer of the Guards, I expect,' continued my tireless interrogator.

'That's enough of your chatter,' the captain's wife said to him. 'You can see that the young man is tired after his journey; he can't be bothered with listening to you . . . Hold your hands straighter now . . . And you, my good sir,' she continued, turning to me, 'you mustn't grieve at being sent to this God-forsaken place. You are not the first, and you won't be the last. You will grow to like it after a time. Shvabrin – Alexei Ivanytch – was transferred to us five years ago for manslaughter. Heaven knows what made him do it; you see, he went out of town with a lieutenant; they both took their swords with them and soon started to prod each other, and Alexei Ivanytch stabbed the lieutenant – before a couple of witnesses at that! Well, there you are – the most learned are liable to err.'

At that moment, the sergeant, a well-built young Cossack, entered the room.

'Maximytch,' the captain's wife addressed him, 'find

some quarters for this officer and make sure that they're clean.'

'As you say, Vassilissa Yegorovna,' the sergeant replied. 'Could his Honour not lodge at Ivan Polezhayev's?'

'Don't talk nonsense, Maximytch,' said the captain's wife, 'Polezhayev's is crowded out as it is; anyway, he's a friend of mine and remembers that we are his superiors. Take the officer . . . what is your name, my dear sir?'

'Pyotr Andreitch.'

'Take Pyotr Andreitch to Semyon Kuzov's. It was he, the rascal, who allowed his horse into my kitchen-garden. Well, and is everything in order, Maximytch?'

'Everything's all right, heaven be thanked!' the Cossack replied. 'Only Corporal Prokhorov had a fight in the bath-house with Ustinya Negulina over a tub of hot water.'

'Ivan Ignatyitch,' said the captain's wife to the one-eyed old man, 'find out which of the two, Prokhorov or Ustinya, is to blame and then punish them both. Well, Maximytch, go now and may God be with you. Pyotr Andreitch, Maximytch will accompany you to your quarters.'

I bowed and took my leave. The sergeant led me to a cottage standing on the steep bank of the river at the extreme end of the fortress. One half of the cottage was occupied by the family of Semyon Kuzov, and the other half was given over for my own use. It consisted of one fairly clean room, divided into two by a partition. Savyelitch began to unpack while I stood looking out of the narrow window. The gloomy steppe stretched away before me. On one side stood a few small cottages; several chickens were wandering about in the street. An old woman, standing on the steps with a trough in her hands, was calling to some pigs,

who were answering her with good-natured grunts.
And this was the spot in which I was fated to spend my
youth! I was overcome by dejection; I came away from
the window and went to bed without any supper, in
spite of the exhortations of Savyelitch, who kept
repeating:

'Good Lord above! He won't eat anything! What
will the mistress say if the child is taken ill?'

The following morning, I had only just finished
dressing when the door opened and a young officer,
short and with a swarthy, extremely ugly but most
lively face, entered my room.

'Forgive me,' he said in French, 'for coming so in-
formally to make your acquaintance. I learned yesterday of your arrival; the desire to see at last a new
human face so overwhelmed me that I lost patience.
You will understand this when you have lived here a
little longer.'

I guessed that this was the officer who had been
dismissed from the Guards for duelling. We quickly
became acquainted. Shvabrin was certainly no fool.
His conversation was sharp and entertaining. He gave
me a most hilarious description of the commandant's
family and friends, and the spot to which fate had
brought me. I was laughing fit to burst when the same
old soldier who had been mending his uniform in the
commandant's front hall came into the room with an
invitation from Vassilissa Yegorovna to dine with her
and her husband. Shvabrin volunteered to go with me.

Approaching the commandant's house, we saw on
the square about twenty old soldiers with long pig-
tails and three-cornered hats. They were standing to
attention. Before them stood the commandant, a tall,
vigorous old man in a night-cap and nankeen dressing-
gown. Seeing us, he came up, said a few kind words to
me, and then continued to drill his men. We were

going to stop and watch, but he asked us to go and join Vassilissa Yegorovna, promising that he would follow us.

'There's nothing for you to see here,' he added.

Vassilissa Yegorovna received us simply and cordially and treated me as if she had known me all her life. The old soldier and Palashka were laying the table.

'And what's keeping my Ivan Kuzmitch so long at his drill today?' said the commandant's wife. 'Palashka, call your master in to dinner. And where is Masha?'

At that point a girl of about eighteen entered the room; she had a round, rosy face and light-brown hair, combed smoothly away behind her ears, which had gone quite red with embarrassment. I did not take to her very much at first sight. I looked at her with prejudiced eyes: Shvabrin had described Masha, the captain's daughter, as a perfect little fool to me. Marya Ivanovna sat down in a corner and began to sew. In the meantime, the cabbage-soup was brought in. Vassilissa Yegorovna, seeing that her husband was still absent, sent Palashka for a second time to fetch him.

'Tell your master that the guests are waiting and that the soup will get cold. Thank heaven the drill isn't going to run away; he'll have plenty of time to shout himself hoarse later on.'

The captain soon appeared, accompanied by the little one-eyed old man.

'What's been keeping you, my dear?' his wife said to him. 'The food's been ready an age, and yet you wouldn't come in.'

'But I was taken up with my service duties, Vassilissa Yegorovna,' replied Ivan Kuzmitch: 'I was instructing my soldiers.'

'That'll do!' retorted the captain's wife. 'It's all a lot of chatter about your instructing the soldiers; they're not fit for the Service and you don't know the first thing about it either. You would do better to stay at home and pray to God. My dear guests, please take your seats at the table.'

We sat down to dinner. Vassilissa Yegorovna never stopped talking for a single moment and overwhelmed me with questions. Who were my parents? Were they alive? Where did they live, and how much were they worth? On hearing that my father had three hundred serfs, she exclaimed:

'Fancy that now! There really are some rich people in the world! And we, my dear, have only got the one maid, Palashka; but, thank God, we live well enough. Masha is a problem though – she's of marriageable age, but what has she got for a dowry? A fine tooth-comb, a broom and three copecks (God forgive me!) for a visit to the bath-house. It's all right if she can find a good man; if not, however, she'll have to resign herself to being left on the shelf.'

I glanced at Marya Ivanovna; she had blushed all over, and tears were even dropping into her plate. I felt sorry for her, and hastened to change the conversation.

'I have heard,' I said somewhat inconsequentially, 'that the Bashkirs* are forming up for an attack on your fortress.'

'Whom did you hear that from, sir?' asked Ivan Kuzmitch.

'I was told so in Orenburg,' I replied.

'It's all rubbish!' said the commandant. 'We've heard nothing of them for a long time. The Bashkirs are a frightened lot now, and the Kirghiz† have been taught a lesson, too. Have no fear that they'll attack us; if they tried anything like that, I'd give them such a

---

* Turco-mongolian tribe inhabiting region north of Orenburg between the river Kama and the Urals.
† Kazakh (at the time wrongly called Kirghiz), a Turkic nomadic tribe living in the region east of the Ural river.

ticking off as would keep them quiet for the next ten years.'

'And aren't you frightened,' I said, turning to the captain's wife, 'to remain in a fortress which is exposed to such dangers?'

'It's just a question of habit, my dear,' she replied. 'Twenty years ago, when we were transferred here from the regiment – heavens above, how terrified I was of those accursed infidels! If I happened to catch a glimpse of their lynx caps, or if I heard their shrieking – believe me, my heart would freeze! But now I have got so used to it that I wouldn't move a fraction if someone were to tell me that the villains were prowling round the fortress.'

'Vassilissa Yegorovna is a very brave woman,' Shvabrin observed solemnly. 'Ivan Kuzmitch can bear witness to that.'

'Yes, indeed,' said Ivan Kuzmitch, 'my wife isn't one of the timid sort.'

'And Marya Ivanovna?' I asked. 'Is she also as brave as you?'

'Masha brave?' her mother replied. 'No, Masha is a coward. Even now, she can't bear to hear the report of a gun; it makes her tremble all over like a leaf. And when, two years ago, Ivan Kuzmitch took it into his head to fire our cannon on my name-day, the little darling nearly died of fright. Since that date we've never fired the accursed cannon again.'

We rose from the table. The captain and his wife went off to lie down; I went to Shvabrin's quarters, where we spent the whole evening together.

4. The Duel

Right then, take up your stance,
And you will see how I shall run your
person through!

KNYAZHNIN: *The Odd Fellows*

Several weeks passed and my life in the Belogorsky fortress became not only endurable, but even pleasant. I was received as one of the family in the commandant's house. Both husband and wife were most worthy people. Ivan Kuzmitch, who had risen from the ranks, was a simple, uneducated man, but extremely honest and kind. His wife ruled him, which suited his easy-going nature. Vassilissa Yegorovna looked upon the affairs of the Service in the same way as she regarded her own household duties and controlled the fortress as she did her own home. Marya Ivanovna soon ceased to be shy with me. We became friends. I found her a sensible and feeling girl. Imperceptibly, I grew attached to this kind family and even to Ivan Ignatyitch, the one-eyed garrison lieutenant, for whom Shvabrin had invented an illicit relationship with Vassilissa Yegorovna, an accusation devoid of even a vestige of truth; however, Shvabrin did not worry about that.

I received my commission. My service duties were no burden to me. In this God-protected fortress, there were neither parades, nor drill nor guard-duty. The commandant sometimes instructed the soldiers for his own amusement; but he had not yet been able to teach all of them the difference between their right and left hands, although many, so as not to make a mistake, crossed themselves at each turn. Shvabrin owned several French books. I began to read them, and a taste for literature awakened in me. In the mornings I read, practised translating, and sometimes wrote verse. I almost always dined at the commandant's, where I usually spent the rest of the day and whither, sometimes of an evening, Father Gerassim repaired with his wife, Akulina Pamfilovna, the biggest gossip in the entire neighbourhood. Alexei Ivanytch Shvabrin, needless to say, I saw every day; his conversation, however, I found increasingly less agreeable. His incessant jokes at the expense of the commandant's family greatly displeased me, and in particular, his sarcastic comments about Marya Ivanovna. There was no other society in the fortress, and I wished for no other.

In spite of the predictions, the Bashkirs did not rise. Peace reigned over our fortress. But this peace was suddenly interrupted by internal dissension.

I have already mentioned that I was occupying myself with literature. My attempts, for those days, were tolerable, and Alexandr Petrovitch Sumarokov praised them highly a few years later. One day I succeeded in writing a song which greatly satisfied me. It is well-known that authors, under pretext of seeking advice, sometimes attempt to find a benevolent listener. And so, having written my song, I took it to Shvabrin, the only person in the whole fortress with any poetical appreciation. After a few introductory words, I drew my notebook from my pocket and read him the following lines:

> *I banish thoughts of love and try*
> *My fair one to forget;*
> *And to be free again I fly*
> *From Masha with regret.*

But wheresoever I may go,
Those eyes I still do see.
My troubled soul no peace may know,
There is no rest for me.

Oh, when thou dost learn my torment,
Pity, Masha, oh pity me!
My cruel fate is plain to see –
I am prisoner held by thee.

'What do you think of it?' I asked Shvabrin, expecting the praise I certainly felt entitled to. But to my great irritation, Shvabrin, who was usually pretty indulgent, resolutely announced that my song was bad.

'Why?' I asked him, concealing my annoyance.

'Because,' he replied, 'such verses are of the kind my tutor, Vasily Kirilitch Tredyakovsky,* would write, and remind me very much of his love couplets.'

Here he took my notebook from me and mercilessly began to tear every verse and every word to bits, sneering at me in the most sarcastic fashion. I could not stand it, and tearing my book from his hands, I told him that I would never again show him my verses. Shvabrin made fun of this threat, too.

'We'll see,' he said, 'if you keep your word. Every poet needs an audience, just as Ivan Kuzmitch needs his quota of vodka before dinner. And who is this Masha, to whom you confess your tender passion and amorous grief? Not Marya Ivanovna by any chance?'

'It's none of your business,' I replied, frowning, 'who this Masha is. I ask neither for your opinion nor for your conjectures.'

---

* Vasily Tredyakovsky (1703–69), minor poet, translator and scientist, author of *New and Brief Method of Russian Versemaking.*

'Oho, the proud poet and discreet lover!' Shvabrin continued, irritating me more and more. 'But listen to the advice of a friend: if you wish to succeed, don't write songs.'

'What do you mean, sir? Be good enough to explain yourself.'

'With pleasure. I mean that if you wish that Masha Mironov should meet you at dusk, give her, instead of your tender verses, a pair of earrings.'

My blood boiled.

'Why do you have such an opinion of her?' I asked, with difficulty restraining my indignation.

'Because,' he replied with a devilish smile, 'I know her nature and habits from experience.'

'You're lying, you scoundrel!' I exclaimed with rage. 'You're lying in the most shameless fashion.'

Shvabrin's expression changed.

'That will not be overlooked,' he said, gripping my hand. 'You will give me satisfaction.'

'Certainly. Whenever you wish,' I replied, delighted.

At that moment I was ready to tear him to pieces.

I instantly made my way to Ivan Ignatyitch, whom I found with a needle in his hand: the commandant's wife had charged him with the task of threading mushrooms to be dried for use in winter.

'Ah, welcome, Pyotr Andreitch!' he said, seeing me. 'For what purpose has God brought you here, may I ask?'

Briefly I explained that I had had a quarrel with Alexei Ivanytch, and that I had come to ask him, Ivan Ignatyitch, to be my second. Ivan Ignatyitch listened attentively, staring at me with his single eye.

'You mean to say,' he said, 'that you want to kill Alexei Ivanytch, and that you would like me to be a witness to it? Is that so, may I ask?'

'Exactly so.'

'Mercy on us, Pyotr Andreitch! Whatever are you thinking of? You've quarrelled with Alexei Ivanytch – a great misfortune! Words do no injury. He has insulted you, and you have given it to him hot; he gives you a punch on the nose, you give him a box on the ear, another, a third – and then each goes his own way; before long we make peace between the two of you. Is it right to kill one's fellow man, may I ask? If you did kill Alexei Ivanytch – all right; I wouldn't care much; I'm not too keen on him myself. But what if he were to run you through? What then? Who would be the loser then, may I ask?'

The logic of the sensible lieutenant had no effect on me. I held to my intention.

'As you wish,' said Ivan Ignatyitch. 'Do as you like. But why should I be a witness to it? To what purpose? People fight, but what's so wonderful about that, may I ask? Heaven be thanked, I have fought against the Swedes and the Turks, and I have seen enough fighting!'

I tried to explain to him as best I could the duties of a second, but Ivan Ignatyitch could not understand me at all.

'Do as you wish,' he said, 'but if I am to be involved in this affair, it will be to go to Ivan Kuzmitch and report to him, as is my duty, that a crime against the interests of the State is being plotted within the fortress, and to ask him to take the necessary measures . . .'

I became alarmed and besought Ivan Ignatyitch not to say anything about it to the commandant; I persuaded him with difficulty; he gave me his word, and I gave up the idea of seeking his active assistance.

As usual, I spent the evening at the commandant's house. I tried to appear gay and indifferent, so as to arouse no suspicion and to avoid a lot of troublesome questions; but I confess that I did not share that coolness which people in my position almost always boast about. That evening I felt disposed to be tender and emotional. I found Marya Ivanovna more than usually attractive. The thought that perhaps I was seeing her for the last time endowed her, in my eyes, with something rather touching. Shvabrin was there too. I took him aside and informed him of my conversation with Ivan Ignatyitch.

'Why should we have seconds?' he said drily. 'We can do without them.'

We agreed to fight behind the haystacks near the fortress, and to be there by seven o'clock the next morning. We appeared to be conversing together in such a friendly fashion that Ivan Ignatyitch nearly let the cat out of the bag in his joy.

'You should have arrived at that long ago,' he said to me with a satisfied expression. 'A bad peace is better than a good quarrel, and an unscarred body more important than honour.'

'What's that, Ivan Ignatyitch?' said the commandant's wife, who was sitting in the corner, telling her fortune by the cards. 'What's that? I did not hear you.'

Ivan Ignatyitch, noting my signs of displeasure and remembering his promise, grew confused and did not know how to reply. Shvabrin came to his rescue.

'Ivan Ignatyitch,' he said, 'approves our reconciliation.'

'And with whom have you been quarrelling, my dear?'

'I had quite a serious row with Pyotr Andreitch.'

'What about?'

'The merest trifle – about a song, Vassilissa Yegorovna.'

'What a thing to quarrel about – a song! How did it happen?'

'In this way: not long ago Pyotr Andreitch composed a song, and while he was singing it to me today, I struck up with my favourite ditty:

> *Captain's daughter, oh captain's daughter,*
> *Walk not out at the midnight hour.*

'Discord arose. Pyotr Andreitch became angry, but then considered that everyone is free to sing what he likes, and there the matter ended.'

Shvabrin's brazenness nearly sent me out of my mind with fury; nobody but myself, however, understood his coarse insinuations – at any rate, nobody paid any attention to them. From songs the conversation turned to poets, and the commandant observed that they were all utterly dissolute and terrible drunkards, and advised me, as a friend, to give up writing verse, since such activities did not go with service life and led to nothing good.

Shvabrin's presence was intolerable to me. I soon took leave of the commandant and his family; when I got home, I examined my sword, tested its point and went to bed, after giving Savyelitch instructions to wake me soon after six o'clock.

At the appointed hour on the following morning, I stood behind the haystacks awaiting my adversary. He soon appeared.

'We may be disturbed,' he said to me, 'so we'll have to be quick.'

We took off our uniforms and, wearing our waistcoats only, we drew our swords. At that moment Ivan Ignatyitch, with about five old soldiers, suddenly appeared from behind a haystack. He summoned us to the commandant. Unwillingly, we obeyed him; the soldiers surrounded us and we set off for the fortress, following Ivan Ignatyitch who, walking with extreme importance, led us in triumph.

We entered the commandant's house. Ivan Ignatyitch opened the door, and announced triumphantly:

'Here they are!'

Vassilissa Yegorovna met us.

'Ah, my good men! Now what's all this about? How?
What? You planned to commit murder in our fortress?
Ivan Kuzmitch, place them under arrest immediately!
Pyotr Andreitch, Alexei Ivanytch, surrender your
swords this instant! Hand them over now, hand them
over! Palashka, take these swords into the lumber-
room. Pyotr Andreitch, I did not expect this of you!
Aren't you ashamed of yourself? It's all right for
Alexei Ivanytch – he was expelled from the Guards for
killing a man, and he does not believe in God. But you?
Do you wish to follow in his footsteps?'

Ivan Kuzmitch agreed fully with everything his wife
said, and kept saying:

'Yes, indeed, Vassilissa Yegorovna is speaking the
truth. Duels are expressly forbidden by the regulations.'

In the meantime, Palashka took our swords and
carried them off to the lumber-room. I could not help
bursting out laughing. Shvabrin preserved his solemnity.

'With all due respect to you,' he said to her coldly,
'I cannot but observe that you cause yourself unneces-
sary trouble in setting yourself up as our judge. Leave
it to Ivan Kuzmitch – it is his affair.'

'Ah, my good sir,' retorted the commandant's wife,
'are not husband and wife one in spirit and flesh? Ivan
Kuzmitch, what are you gaping at? Have them
separated at once and placed under arrest on bread and
water until they've regained their proper senses. Then
let Father Gerassim impose a penance on them, that
they may pray to God for forgiveness and repent before
all men.'

Ivan Kuzmitch did not know what to do. Marya Ivanovna was extremely pale. Little by little the storm abated; the commandant's wife calmed down and forced us to embrace one another. Palashka brought us back our swords. We left the commandant's house apparently reconciled. Ivan Ignatyitch accompanied us.

'Aren't you ashamed of yourself?' I asked angrily. 'Reporting us to the commandant after giving your word that you wouldn't?'

'As God is holy, I didn't say a word of it to Ivan Kuzmitch!' he replied. 'Vassilissa Yegorovna wormed it out of me. She arranged everything without the commandant knowing. Anyway, heaven be thanked that it has ended as it has!'

With these words he turned home and Shvabrin and I were left alone.

'Our affair cannot end here,' I said to him.

'Of course not,' replied Shvabrin. 'You will have to answer with your blood for your insolence; but they'll probably be keeping an eye on us. We will have to dissemble for a few days. Good-bye.'

And we parted as if nothing had happened.

Returning to the commandant's house, I sat down, as usual, near Marya Ivanovna. Ivan Kuzmitch was not at home. Vassilissa Yegorovna was occupied with household affairs. We conversed in an undertone. Marya Ivanovna reproached me tenderly for the anxiety my quarrel with Shvabrin had caused them all.

'I nearly fainted,' she said, 'when I heard that you intended to fight with swords. How strange men are! For a single word which they would probably forget in a week, they are ready to murder each other and sacrifice not only their lives but their consciences, and the happiness of those who . . . But I am sure that you were not the cause of the quarrel. Alexei Ivanytch was doubtless to blame.'

'And why do you think that, Marya Ivanovna?'

'Because . . . because he is so sarcastic. I do not like Alexei Ivanytch. I find him very repulsive, and yet, strangely enough, not for anything would I have him dislike me. It would worry me dreadfully.'

'And what do you think, Marya Ivanovna? Does he like you or not?'

Marya Ivanovna stammered and blushed.

'It seems to me . . .' she said, '. . . I think he does like me.'

'Why do you think that?'

'Because he asked me to marry him.'

'Marry! He asked you to marry him! When?'

'Last year. Two months before you arrived.'

'And you refused?'

'As you can see. Alexei Ivanytch, of course, is an intelligent man, of good family and rich; but when I think that I should have to kiss him beneath the crown* before everyone . . . no, not for anything!'

Marya Ivanovna's words opened my eyes and explained many things to me. I now understood the persistent calumny with which Shvabrin pursued her. He had probably noticed our mutual attraction and had tried to turn us against each other. The words which had brought about our quarrel seemed all the more base to me when I recognized that they were not coarse, indecent mockery, but premeditated slander. My desire to chastise the insolent traducer became yet stronger within me, and I impatiently awaited a favourable opportunity to do so.

I did not have to wait long. The next day, as I sat composing an elegy and biting my pen in search of a rhyme, Shvabrin tapped at my window. I put my pen down, took up my sword and went out to him.

* As part of the marriage ceremony, bride and bridegroom kissed beneath crowns held above their heads.

'Why delay any further?' Shvabrin said to me; 'nobody's watching us. Let's go down to the river. We won't be disturbed there.'

We set off in silence. Stepping down a winding path, we stopped at the edge of the river and drew our swords. Shvabrin was more skilful than I, but I was stronger and more daring, and Monsieur Beaupré, who had once been a soldier, had given me several lessons in fencing, which I turned to good account. Shvabrin had not expected to find in me so dangerous an opponent. For a long time neither gave the other the opportunity to do any injury; at length, noticing that Shvabrin was weakening, I began to bear down upon him vigorously and almost forced him into the river itself. Suddenly I heard my name being loudly called. I glanced round and saw Savyelitch running down the steep path towards me. . . . At that same moment, I felt a sharp jab in my chest, just beneath my right shoulder; I fell and lost consciousness.

5. Love

Ah, you maiden, pretty maiden!
Do not marry while you are yet so young;
You must ask your father, ask your
    mother;
Father, mother and all your kin;
Gather, maiden, wisdom and intelligence;
Wisdom and intelligence: these shall be
    your dowry.   FOLK SONG

If you find one better than me, you'll
    forget me,
Worse than me, and you'll remember.
                    FOLK SONG

On recovering consciousness, I was unable for some
time to collect my senses or understand what had happened to me. I was lying in bed in a strange room and
felt extremely weak. Savyelitch was standing before
me with a candle in his hand. Somebody was carefully
unwinding the bandages which had been bound round
my chest and shoulders. Gradually my thoughts
cleared. I remembered the duel and guessed that I had
been wounded. At that moment the door creaked.

'Well, how is he?' whispered a voice which sent a
tremor through my body.

'Still in the same condition,' replied Savyelitch with
a sigh. 'Still unconscious, and this is the fifth day now.'

I tried to turn my head but could not.

'Where am I? Who's there?' I said with an effort.

Marya Ivanovna came up to the bed and bent over
me.

'Well, and how are you feeling?' she said.

'Heaven be thanked!' I replied in a weak voice. 'Is
that you, Marya Ivanovna? Tell me . . .'

I had not the strength to continue and fell silent. Savyelitch gave a cry and his face lit up with joy.

'He has come to himself, he has come to himself!' he repeated. 'Thanks be to Thee, good Lord! Well, Pyotr Andreitch, my dear, what a fright you gave me! It was no joke – five days! . . .'

Marya Ivanovna interrupted him.

'Don't talk to him too much, Savyelitch,' she said. 'He's still weak.'

She went out and closed the door softly behind her. My thoughts were in a turmoil. And so I was in the commandant's house: Marya Ivanovna had been in to see me. I wanted to ask Savyelitch some questions but the old man shook his head and stopped up his ears. Vexed, I closed my eyes and soon fell asleep.

When I awoke, I called Savyelitch, but instead of him, I saw Marya Ivanovna standing before me. She greeted me in her angelic voice. I cannot describe the delightful sensation which took hold of me at that moment. I seized her hand and pressed it to me, watering it with tears of emotion. Masha did not withdraw it . . . and suddenly her lips touched my cheek and I felt their hot, fresh kiss. A surge of fire ran through me.

'Dear, good Marya Ivanovna,' I said to her, 'be my wife, consent to make me happy.'

She regained her composure.

'For Heaven's sake, keep calm,' she said, removing her hand from mine. 'You're not out of danger yet: your wound may reopen. Look after yourself, if only for my sake.'

With these words she left, leaving me in an ecstasy of bliss. Happiness revived me. She will be mine! She loves me! This thought filled my entire being.

From that moment I grew hourly better. The regimental barber – there was no other doctor in the fortress – treated my wound, and thank heaven, he did not try to be too clever. Youth and nature accelerated my recovery. I was nursed by the commandant's whole family. Marya Ivanovna never left my side. It goes without saying that at the first favourable opportunity I took up my interrupted declaration of love, and Marya Ivanovna listened to me with greater patience. Without any affectation she confessed her attachment to me, and said that her parents would undoubtedly be pleased at her happiness.

'But think it over well,' she added: 'won't there be some opposition on the part of your parents?'

I considered the matter. Of my mother's affection I had no doubts but, knowing my father's nature and way of thinking, I felt that my love would not move him very much and that he would regard it as a young man's fancy. I candidly confessed this to Marya Ivanovna but resolved, all the same, to write to my father as eloquently as I could and implore his paternal blessing. I showed the letter to Marya Ivanovna, who found it so convincing and moving that she had no doubts as to its success and abandoned herself to the feelings of her tender heart with all the confidence of youth and love.

I made peace with Shvabrin in the first days of my recovery. Ivan Kuzmitch, in reprimanding me for the duel, said:

'Well, I should really put you under arrest, Pyotr Andreitch, but you have been punished enough already without that. Alexei Ivanytch, however, I have placed under guard in the granary, and Vassilissa Yegorovna has got his sword under lock and key. It'll give him time to think it over and repent.'

I was too happy to cherish any feelings of hostility in my heart. I began to intercede for Shvabrin, and the good commandmant agreed with his wife in deciding to set him free. Shvabrin called on me; he expressed deep regret for what had happened between us, confessed that he was entirely to blame and besought me to forget the past. Not being a resentful person by nature, I sincerely forgave him for the quarrel, and the wound I had received at his hands. I attributed his calumny to the vexation of wounded vanity and slighted love and magnanimously pardoned my unhappy rival.

I was soon well again and able to return to my own quarters. I impatiently awaited an answer to my letter, not daring to hope and trying to suppress my sad forebodings. I had not yet mentioned the matter to Vassilissa Yegorovna and her husband; my proposal, however, would come as no surprise to them. Neither I nor Marya Ivanovna made any attempt to conceal our feelings from them, and we felt certain of their consent beforehand.

At last one morning Savyelitch came into my room with a letter in his hand. I seized it with trembling fingers. The address was written in my father's hand. This prepared me for something important since it was usually my mother who wrote to me, he merely adding a few lines at the end.

For a long time I could not unseal the packet, but kept on reading the solemn superscription:

> *To my son, Pyotr Andreyevitch Grinev,*
> *The Belogorsky Fortress,*
> *The Province of Orenburg.*

I attempted to divine from the handwriting the mood in which the letter had been written. At last I resolved to open it and saw from the first few lines that all my hopes were lost. The letter read as follows:

My son Pyotr,
Your letter, in which you ask us for our parental blessing and consent to your marriage with Marya Ivanovna,

*Mironov's daughter, reached us on the 15th of this
month, and not only do I not intend to give you either
my blessing or consent, but I propose to come and teach
you a lesson for your pranks, as I would a small boy,
in spite of your officer's rank; for you have shown that
you are not yet worthy to carry the sword, entrusted to
you for the defence of our native country and not for
the purpose of fighting duels with other madcaps like
yourself. I shall write instantly to Andrei Karlovitch,
asking him to transfer you from the Belogorsky fortress
to some place further away, where you will be cured
of your folly. Your mother, on hearing the news of your
duel and that you have been wounded, fell ill with grief
and now lies in bed. What will become of you? I pray
God that you will mend your ways, although I do not
dare to hope in His great mercy.*

Your father, A.G.

The reading of this letter aroused various feelings
within me. The harsh expressions so unsparingly used
by my father wounded me deeply. The disdain with
which he referred to Marya Ivanovna seemed to me to
be as unbecoming as it was unjust. The thought of my
being transferred from the Belogorsky fortress appalled
me, but the thing that grieved me most of all was the
news of my mother's illness. I felt indignant with
Savyelitch and had no doubt that it was he who had
told my parents of my duel. After pacing up and down
my narrow room, I stopped in front of him and said
with a menacing look:

'It seems that you are not content that, thanks to
you, I should be wounded and at death's door for a
whole month; you wish to kill my mother as well.'

Savyelitch looked thunderstruck.

'In heaven's name, master,' he said, 'what do you
mean? My fault that you were wounded? As God is my

witness, I was running to shield you with my own
chest from Alexi Ivanytch's sword! It was my age –
curse it – that prevented me! But what have I done to
your mother?'

'What have you done?' I replied. 'Who asked you to
write back and inform against me? Have you been
placed here to spy on me?'

'I wrote back and informed against you?' Savyelitch
replied tearfully. 'Heavenly Father! Be pleased to read
what my master has written to me: then you will see
how I informed against you.'

He drew a letter from his pocket and I read the
following:

*You should be ashamed of yourself, you old dog, for
ignoring my strict instructions that you should write to
me about my son, Pyotr Andreyevitch, and for leaving
it to strangers to tell me of his pranks. Is this how you
fulfil your duty and the will of your master? I will send
you to tend pigs, you old dog, for concealing the truth
and indulging the young man. On receipt of this, I
order you to write back to me instantly and inform me
of the present state of his health which, I am told, is
better; also of the exact place of his wound and whether
he has been properly looked after.*

It was clear that Savyelitch was completely innocent
and that I had been wrong to insult him with my
reproaches and suspicions. I asked his forgiveness, but
the old man was inconsolable.

'That I should have lived to see this!' he kept on
repeating. 'These are the thanks I receive from my
masters! I am an old dog, and a swineherd and the
cause of your wound as well! No, my dear Pyotr
Andreitch, it is not I, but that accursed "Monsoo"
who is to blame: it was he who taught you to thrust
with those iron spits and to stamp your feet, as if by

thrusting and stamping you could protect yourself
from a wicked man! And we had to take on that
"Monsoo" and throw good money down the drain!'

But who was it then who had taken it upon himself
to inform my father of my behaviour? The general?
But he had shown extremely little interest in me, and
Ivan Kuzmitch had not considered it necessary to
report my duel to him. I was lost in conjectures. My
suspicions finally rested on Shvabrin. He alone would
profit by the denunciation, the consequence of which
could be my removal from the fortress and my separation from the commandant's family. I went off to tell
Marya Ivanovna everything. She met me on the steps.

'What's happened to you?' she said when she saw
me. 'How pale you are!'

'It's all over,' I replied, and I handed her my father's
letter.

She in turn grew pale. Having read the letter, she
returned it to me with a trembling hand and said in
an unsteady voice:

'It was clearly not for me . . . Your parents do not
want me in your family. In all things may God's will
be done! God knows better than we what is good for
us. There's nothing to be done, Pyotr Andreitch; may
you at any rate be happy . . .'

'This is not to be!' I cried, seizing her hand. 'You
love me; I am prepared for anything. Let us go and
throw ourselves at your parents' feet; they are simple
people, not hard-hearted and proud . . . They will give
us their blessing; we will be married . . . And then, in
time, I'm sure we'll gain my father's approval; my
mother will be on our side; he will forgive me . . .'

'No, Pyotr Andreitch,' Masha replied. 'I will not
marry you without your parents' blessing. Without it
you would never be happy. Let us submit to the will of
God. If you find the one destined for you, if you grow

to love another – God be with you, Pyotr Andreitch; I will pray for you both . . .'

She burst into tears and left me; I wanted to follow her into her room, but I felt in no condition to control myself, and therefore returned home.

I was sitting in my room, plunged in deep thought, when Savyelitch suddenly interrupted my reflections.

'Here, master,' he said, handing me a written sheet of paper. 'See whether I am here to inform against my master, or to try to stir up trouble between father and son.'

I took the paper from his hand: it was Savyelitch's answer to the letter he had received. Here it is, word for word:

Dear Sir, Andrei Petrovitch, our gracious father!

I have received your gracious letter in which you are pleased to be angry with me, your servant, telling me that I should be ashamed of myself for not fulfilling my master's orders; but I am not an old dog but your faithful servant, and I do obey my master's orders, and I have always served you zealously to my grey hairs. I did not write to you about Pyotr Andreitch's wound, because I did not wish to alarm you for no reason, and I hear that the mistress, our mother Avdotya Vassilyevna took to her bed with fright and I will pray to God for her recovery. Pyotr Andreitch was wounded under the right shoulder, in the chest, immediately beneath the bone to the depth of one and a half vershoks,* and he was put to bed in the commandant's house whither we carried him from the river-bank, and the local barber, Stepan Paramonov, treated him; and now, Pyotr Andreitch, thank God, is well, and I have nothing but good to write about him. I have heard that his superior officers are satisfied with him; and Vassilissa Yegorovna

---

*One vershok equals one and three-quarter inches.

treats him as if he were her own son. And as for the
incident that happened to him, the young man should
not be reproached: a horse has four legs and yet it
stumbles. It also pleased you to write that you will send
me to tend pigs; be that your master's will. Herewith I
humbly bow before you.

> *Your faithful serf, Arkhip Savyelitch.*

I could not help smiling occasionally as I read the
good old man's letter. I was in no condition to write an
answer to my father, and Savyelitch's letter seemed
sufficient to calm my mother's fears.

From that time my position changed. Marya
Ivanovna scarcely ever spoke to me and in every way
tried to avoid me. The commandant's house became
hateful to me. I gradually grew accustomed to sitting
by myself at home. Vassilissa Yegorovna reproached
me for this at first but, noticing my obstinacy, she
left me in peace. I only saw Ivan Kuzmitch when the
Service demanded it. I rarely met Shvabrin, and then
unwillingly, the more so since I noticed his veiled
antipathy towards me, which confirmed me in my
suspicions. My life became intolerable. I fell into a state
of gloomy brooding, which was fed by loneliness and
inaction. My love grew stronger in solitude and became
more and more oppressive to me. I lost the desire for
reading and literature. My spirits sank. I feared that I
would either go out of my mind or give way to dissipation. Unexpected events, which were to have an important influence on my whole life, suddenly gave my
soul a powerful and salutary shock.

6. The Pugachev Rising

Listen then, my young lads,
To what we, the old ones, will tell you.
SONG

Before proceeding to a description of the strange events
of which I was a witness, I must say a few words
concerning the situation in the province of Orenburg
at the end of the year 1773.

This vast and rich province was inhabited by a
number of half-savage peoples, who had but recently
acknowledged the sovereignty of the Russian Tsars.
Their continual risings, their unfamiliarity with laws
and civic life, their thoughtlessness and cruelty
demanded ceaseless vigilance on the part of the Government to keep them in subjection. Fortresses had been
erected in suitable places and were garrisoned to a large
extent by Cossacks, who had long since held possession
of the banks of the Yaik. But these Yaikian Cossacks,
whose duty it was to preserve peace and watch over the
security of the district, had for some time themselves
been a source of anxiety and danger to the Government. In 1772 an insurrection broke out in their
principal township. It was caused by the stern measures
taken by Major-General Traubenberg* to enforce
dutiful obedience from the troops. The outcome was
the barbarous murder of Traubenberg, self-appointed
changes in the administration and eventually the
suppression of the revolt by cannon-shot and cruel
punishments.

This occurred a short while before my arrival at the

---

* Well known for his cruelty and eventually killed by the Cossacks
in the Pugachev Uprising.

Belogorsky fortress. All was now quiet, or so it seemed; the authorities had too readily believed in the pretended repentance of the cunning rebels, who bore their malice in secret, and only awaited a suitable opportunity for a renewal of the disorders.

I will now return to my story.

One evening (it was at the beginning of October in the year 1773) I was sitting alone at home, listening to the howling of the autumn wind, and staring out of the window at the clouds which raced past the moon. Someone arrived to tell me that I was wanted at the commandant's. I set off immediately for his house. There I found Shvabrin, Ivan Ignatyitch and the Cossack sergeant. Neither Vassilissa Yegorovna nor Marya Ivanovna were in the room. The commandant greeted me with an air of preoccupation. He closed the door, made us all sit down with the exception of the sergeant who was standing by the door and, drawing a paper from his pocket, he said to us:

'Gentlemen, I have important news! Listen to what the general writes.'

He then put on his spectacles and read out the following:

To the commandant of the Belogorsky Fortress, Captain Mironov.

CONFIDENTIAL

I hereby inform you that the fugitive and dissident Don Cossack, Emelyan Pugachev, having committed the unpardonable insolence of assuming the name of the deceased Emperor Peter III,* has collected a band of evilly-disposed persons, has excited a revolt in the Yaikian settlements, and has already taken and des-

---

* 1728–62; grandson of Peter the Great and husband of Catherine the Great, reigned from January to July 1762 when he abdicated, and was later strangled by one of Catherine's many admirers.

troyed several fortresses, looting and murdering on every side. Therefore, on receipt of this, you, Captain, will at once take the necessary measures to repel the above-mentioned villain and pretender, and if possible, to annihilate him totally, should he attack the fortress entrusted to your care.

'Take the necessary measures!' said the commandant, removing his spectacles and folding up the paper. 'As you know, it's easy enough to say. This villain is apparently powerful; and we have only got one hundred and thirty men in all, not counting the Cossacks, upon whom we can place little reliance – don't take that as a reproach, Maximytch.' (The sergeant smiled.) 'Still, we must do the best we can, gentlemen. Ensure that we are prepared and establish guard-duty and night patrols. In the event of an attack, close the gates and assemble the soldiers. You, Maximytch, keep a sharp eye on your Cossacks. Have the cannon inspected and thoroughly cleaned. Most important of all, keep all that I have told you to yourselves, so that nobody in the fortress knows about it beforehand.'

Having given these orders, Ivan Kuzmitch dismissed us. I walked away with Shvabrin, reflecting upon what we had heard.

'How do you think it'll end?' I asked him.

'God knows,' he replied; 'we shall see. At this stage I see nothing to be alarmed about. If, however . . .'

He then became thoughtful and began absent-mindedly to whistle a French air.

In spite of all our precautions, news of the appearance of Pugachev soon spread through the fortress. Ivan Kuzmitch, while having the greatest respect for his wife, would not for anything in the world have confided in her a secret entrusted to him in connection with the Service. On the receipt of the general's letter, he managed fairly skilfully to get Vassilissa Yegorovna out of the way by telling her that Father Gerassim had received some remarkable news from Orenburg, which he was keeping as a great secret. Vassilissa Yegorovna immediately resolved to call on the priest's wife and, on the advice of Ivan Kuzmitch, took Masha with her, lest she should feel bored on her own.

Ivan Kuzmitch, in sole occupation of the house, had instantly sent for us, after locking Palashka in the lumber-room to prevent her from overhearing us.

Vassilissa Yegorovna returned home, without having succeeded in getting anything out of the priest's wife, and learned that Ivan Kuzmitch had held a council during her absence, and that Palashka had been under lock and key. She guessed that her husband had deceived her and immediately set about interrogating him. But Ivan Kuzmitch had prepared himself for the onslaught. Not in the least confused, he replied decisively to his inquisitive consort:

'You see, my dear, the women hereabouts have taken it into their heads to heat their stoves with straw, and since some misfortune might result from this, I have given strict instructions that from now on the women are not to heat their stoves with straw, but should use dry branches and brushwood instead.'

'But why did you have to lock up Palashka then?' asked the commandant's wife. 'Why did the poor girl have to sit in the lumber-room until we returned?'

Ivan Kuzmitch was not prepared for such a question; he became confused and muttered something incoherently. Vassilissa Yegorovna perceived her husband's artfulness but, knowing that she would get nothing out of him, she ceased her questioning and changed the conversation to the pickled cucumbers Akulina Pamfilovna had prepared in some very special way. Vassilissa Yegorovna could not sleep a wink all that night, as she could not guess what was in her husband's mind that she should not be allowed to know.

Returning from mass the following day, she saw Ivan Ignatyitch pulling out of the cannon bits of rag, small stones, wood-chips, knuckle-bones and rubbish of every sort, which had been stuffed into it by the children.

'What can these military preparations mean?' thought the commandant's wife. 'Can it be that they're expecting an attack from the Kirghiz? Surely Ivan Kuzmitch would not hide such trifles from me?'

She called Ivan Ignatyitch, with the firm intention of discovering from him the secret which tormented her feminine curiosity.

Vassilissa Yegorovna made a few observations concerning her household affairs to him, like a judge who begins an investigation with irrelevant questions so as to put the defendant off his guard from the start. Then, after a pause of a few minutes, she sighed deeply, and said, shaking her head:

'Oh, good Lord, what news! What will be the end of it?'

'Oh well, ma'am,' answered Ivan Ignatyitch, 'God is merciful: we have soldiers enough, plenty of powder, and I have cleaned out the cannon. Perhaps we'll manage to repulse Pugachev. Whom God helps nobody can harm.'

'And what sort of a man is this Pugachev?' asked the commandant's wife.

At this point Ivan Ignatyitch perceived that he had said too much and bit his tongue. But it was too late. Vassilissa Yegorovna forced him to tell her everything, after giving him her word that she would not say a word of it to anyone.

Vassilissa Yegorovna kept her promise and said not a word of it to anyone except the priest's wife, and that

merely because her cow was still grazing in the steppe
and might be seized by the villains.

Soon everybody was talking about Pugachev. The
rumours about him varied. The commandant sent his
sergeant to glean as much as he could from the neigh-
bouring villages and fortresses. The sergeant returned
after a couple of days and announced that he had seen
a number of fires in the steppe about sixty versts from
the fortress, and that he had heard from the Bashkirs
that an unknown force was on its way. Beyond that he
could say nothing positive since he had been afraid to
go any further.

Signs of unusual agitation became apparent among
the Cossacks in the fortress; they crowded together in
little groups in all the streets, conversing quietly among
themselves and dispersing at the sight of a dragoon or a
garrison soldier. Spies were sent among them. Yulai, a
Kalmuck converted to Christianity, reported some
important information to the commandant. The sergeant's evidence, according to Yulai, was false; on his
return, the treacherous Cossack had announced to his
comrades that he had been among the rebels and that
he had presented himself to their leader, who had
allowed him to kiss his hand and with whom he had
conversed for a long time. The commandant immediately arrested the sergeant and appointed Yulai in his
place. This change was received by the Cossacks with
manifest displeasure. They murmured loudly and Ivan
Ignatyitch, who saw to it that the commandant's
instructions were carried out, with his own ears heard
them say:

'You'll have it coming to you later, you garrison
rat!'

The commandant had intended interrogating his
prisoner that same day; but the sergeant had escaped
guard, doubtless with the help of his partisans.

A new circumstance served to increase the commandant's anxiety. A Bashkir was caught carrying seditious letters. On this occasion, the commandant again decided to assemble his officers, and for this purpose, he again wished to send away Vassilissa Yegorovna under some plausible pretext. But since Ivan Kuzmitch was a most upright and truthful man, he could think of no other method than that which he had employed on the previous occasion.

'Listen, Vassilissa Yegorovna,' he said to her with a slight cough. 'They say that Father Gerassim has received from the town . . .'

'Enough of that, Ivan Kuzmitch!' the commandant's wife interrupted him. 'It's clear that you propose to assemble a council of war to discuss Emelyan Pugachev without me; you can't fool me!'

Ivan Kuzmitch stared at her.

'Well, my dear,' he said, 'if you know everything already, you may as well stay; we'll talk in front of you.'

'You shouldn't try to be so cunning, my dear,' she replied; 'call for the officers.'

We assembled again. In the presence of his wife, Ivan Kuzmitch read to us Pugachev's proclamation, which had been written by some illiterate Cossack. The outlaw announced his intention of marching at once against our fortress; he invited the Cossacks and the soldiers to join his band and exhorted the commanders to offer no resistance, threatening execution if they did so. The proclamation was written in coarse but powerful language and must have had a dangerous influence on the minds of simple people.

'What an impostor!' exclaimed the commandant's wife. 'That he should dare to make such a proposal to us! To go out and meet him and lay our flags at his feet! Ah, the son of a dog! Surely he knows that we've been forty years in the Service and that, thanks to God, we've seen a thing or two in that time! Surely no commanders have listened to the brigand?'

'I shouldn't have thought so,' Ivan Kuzmitch replied. 'But I've heard that the villain has already taken many fortresses.'

'It certainly seems that he is powerful, then,' observed Shvabrin.

'We shall soon know his real strength,' said the commandant. 'Vassilissa Yegorovna, give me the key to the storehouse. Ivan Ignatyitch, go and bring the Bashkir here, and tell Yulai to fetch the whip.'

'Wait, Ivan Kuzmitch,' said the commandant's wife, rising from the seat. 'Let me take Masha somewhere out of the house; otherwise she'll hear the screaming and be terrified. And I, to tell you the truth, am not keen on being a witness to the torturing. Good-bye for the present.'

In the old days, torture was so rooted in our judicial system that the beneficent edict* ordering its abolition remained for a long time unheeded. It was thought that the criminal's own confession was indispensable for his full conviction – a thought not only illogical, but even totally opposed to sound juridical thinking: for, if the denial of the accused person is not accepted as proof of his innocence, his confession still less should be accepted as proof of his guilt. Even nowadays I sometimes hear old judges regretting the abolition of this barbarous custom. But in those days, nobody, neither the judge nor the accused, doubted the necessity of torture. Thus, the commandant's order caused no alarm or astonishment to any of us. Ivan Ignatyitch went off to fetch the Bashkir, who was under lock and key in the commandant's wife's storehouse, and a few minutes later, the prisoner was led into the hall. The commandant ordered him to be brought before him.

* This edict was instituted by Catherine II.

The Bashkir stepped across the threshold with
difficulty (a block of wood, in the form of stocks, had
been attached to his feet) and removing his tall cap, he
stopped by the door. I looked up at him and shuddered.
Never will I forget that man. He seemed to be over
seventy. He had neither nose nor ears. His head was
shaved; instead of a beard, a few grey hairs sprouted
from his chin; he was small, thin and bent; however,
his narrow little eyes still flashed fire.

'Aha!' said the commandant, recognizing by these
terrible signs one of the rebels punished in the year
1741.* 'It seems that you're an old wolf, and that
you've fallen into our traps before. Apparently it's not
the first time you've rebelled since your nut's so
smoothly planed. Come nearer; tell me who sent you.'

The old Bashkir was silent and looked at the commandant with an utterly vacant expression.

'Why don't you answer?' continued Ivan Kuzmitch.
'Or don't you understand the Russian language? Yulai,
ask him in your own tongue who sent him to our
fortress.'

Yulai repeated Ivan Kuzmitch's question in Tartar.
But the Bashkir looked at him with the same expression
and answered not a word.

'All right, then,' said the commandant. 'I will make
you answer my question. Right, lads, take off that
ridiculous striped gown of his and stroke his back for
him. Yulai, see to it that it's properly done!'

Two old soldiers began to undress the Bashkir. The
unfortunate man's face expressed anxiety. He looked
all around him like a small wild animal caught by
children. When one of the old soldiers seized his hands

* Violent uprisings took place in the district of Bashkiria in the
years 1735–40 and were subdued with incredible cruelty: some
700 villages were burnt down and the noses and ears of the ring-
leaders cut off.

to twine them round his neck, and lifted the old man on to his shoulders, and when Yulai took up the whip and began to brandish it, the Bashkir uttered a weak, imploring groan and, nodding his head, he opened his mouth, in which, in place of a tongue, moved a short stump.

When I reflect that this happened during my lifetime, and that I now live under the mild reign of Emperor Alexander,* I cannot help but feel amazed at the rapid progress of civilization and the spread of the laws of humanity. Young man, if these lines of mine should ever fall into your hands, remember that those changes which come as a result of moral improvements are better and more durable than any which are the outcome of violent events.

We were all horror-stricken.

'Well,' said the commander, 'it's evident that we won't get anything out of him. Yulai, take the Bashkir back to the storehouse. And we, gentlemen, have further matters to discuss.'

We were beginning to consider our situation, when Vassilissa Yegorovna suddenly burst into the room, out of breath and with an expression of extreme alarm.

'What's happened to you?' asked the astonished commandant.

'Very bad news, my dear!' answered Vassilissa Yegorovna. 'Nizhneozerny was captured this morning. Father Gerassim's servant has just got back from there. He saw it being taken. The commandant and all the officers were hanged. All the soldiers were taken prisoner. The villains will be here at any moment.'

This unexpected news came as a great shock to me. The commandant of the Nizhneozerny fortress, a quiet and modest young man, was known to me; a month

* 1777–1825; reigned 1801–25, grandson of Catherine II, son of Paul I, who was murdered with Alexander's knowledge.

or two before, he and his young wife had stayed with
Ivan Kuzmitch while on their way from Orenburg.
Nizhneozerny was twenty-five versts away from our
fortress. We had therefore to expect an attack from
Pugachev at any moment. The fate in store for Marya
Ivanovna came vividly to my mind, and my heart sank
within me.

'Listen, Ivan Kuzmitch,' I said to the commandant.
'Our duty is to defend the fortress to the last breath; of
that no more need be said. But we must consider the
safety of the women. Send them to Orenburg, if the
road is still free, or to some safer, more distant fortress
out of reach of the villains.'

Ivan Kuzmitch turned to his wife and said to her:

'Indeed, my dear, don't you feel that you should go
away until we've settled with the rebels?'

'Nonsense!' said the commandant's wife. 'Name a
fortress safe from bullets. What's wrong with Belogorsky? Thanks to God, we've lived here for twenty-two
years. We've seen the Bashkirs and Kirghiz: perhaps
we'll manage to hold out against Pugachev!'

'Well, my dear,' replied Ivan Kuzmitch, 'stay if you
like, if you have confidence in our fortress. But what
shall we do with Masha? It'll be all right if we can
successfully resist the enemy or hold out until help
comes; but what if the villains capture the fortress?'

'Well, then . . .'

And Vassilissa Yegorovna began to stutter and fell
silent, with an expression of extreme agitation on her
face.

'No, Vassilissa Yegorovna,' continued the commandant, observing that his words had produced an
effect upon her, possibly for the first time in his life.
'It won't do for Masha to stay here. Let us send her to
Orenburg, to her godmother; there are plenty of
soldiers and cannons there and the walls are made of

stone. And I would advise you to go there with her; although you're an old woman, consider what would happen to you if the fortress were taken.'

'All right,' said the commandant's wife; 'so be it: we'll send Masha away. But don't dream of asking me: I won't go. Nothing would make me part with you in my old age, to go and seek a lonely grave in a strange corner of the world. We have lived together, we will die together.'

'That's reasonable enough,' said the commandant. 'But we must hurry. Go and get Masha ready for the journey. We'll send her off before dawn tomorrow, and we'll give her an escort, even though we have no men to spare. But where is Masha?'

'At Akulina Pamfilovna's,' replied the commandan't wife. 'She fainted when she heard of the capture of Nizhneozerny; I am afraid that she might fall ill. Heavens above, to have lived for this!'

Vassilissa Yegorovna went off to prepare her daughter's departure. We continued with our discussions; however, I no longer took any part in them, and did not listen to what was said. Marya Ivanovna appeared at supper, pale and tear-stained. We finished our meal in silence and rose from the table earlier than usual; taking leave of the whole family, we returned to our quarters. But I deliberately forgot my sword and went back for it: I had a feeling that I would find Marya Ivanovna alone. Indeed, she met me in the doorway and handed me my sword.

'Good-bye, Pyotr Andreitch,' she said to me with tears in her eyes; 'they are sending me to Orenburg. Keep well and be happy. Perhaps it will please God to let us see each other again; if not . . .'

And she began to sob. I embraced her.

'Good-bye, my angel,' I said. 'Good-bye, my dear one, my heart's desire! Whatever happens to me, trust that my last thought and my last prayer will be for you!'

Masha sobbed and pressed her head against my chest. I kissed her passionately and hastened out of the room.

7. The Assault

Oh my head, my head,
Oh my head, that has served,
Has served my country well
For three and thirty years,
And yet has obtained for itself,
Neither gold nor joy,
Neither words of praise
Nor rank on high.
All that my head has obtained
Is two upright posts,
With a beech-wood cross-beam,
And a silken noose.

FOLK SONG

That night I neither slept nor undressed. I intended to go at dawn to the fortress gate from which Marya Ivanovna was to leave, and there say good-bye to her for the last time. I felt a great change within myself: my agitation of mind was far less burdensome to me than my recent despondency. Mingled with the grief of separation was vague but sweet hope, an impatient expectation of danger and feelings of noble ambition.

The night slipped by unnoticed. I was on the point of leaving my quarters when the door opened and a corporal came in to announce that our Cossacks had left the fortress during the night, taking Yulai with them by force, and that strange people were riding round the fortress. The thought that Marya Ivanovna would not be able to get away terrified me; I issued a few hasty instructions to the corporal and rushed off at once to the commandant's.

Day had already begun to dawn. I was flying down the street when I heard someone calling me. I stopped.

'Where are you going?' asked Ivan Ignatyitch, over-taking me. 'Ivan Kuzmitch is on the rampart and has sent me to get you. Pugachev has come.'

'Has Marya Ivanovna left?' I asked with a trembling heart.

'No, she was too late,' replied Ivan Ignatyitch. 'The road to Orenburg is cut off; the fortress is surrounded. It looks bad, Pyotr Andreitch!'

We made our way to the rampart, a natural eleva-tion of the ground and fortified by a palisade. All the inhabitants of the fortress were already crowded there. The garrison was under arms. The cannon had been dragged up the rampart the previous day. The com-mandant was walking up and down in front of his meagre ranks. The approach of danger had inspired the old warrior with unusual vigour. Riding up and down the steppe, not far from the fortress, were about twenty horsemen. They seemed to be Cossacks, but among them were also some Bashkirs, easily recogni-zable by their lynx caps and their quivers.

The commandant made the round of his little army, saying to the soldiers:

'Well, children, let us stand firm today for our mother the Empress, and show the whole world that we are brave men, and true to our oaths!'

The soldiers loudly expressed their zeal. Shvabrin stood next to me, looking intently at the enemy. The horsemen riding about the steppe, noticing movement in the fortress, gathered in a little cluster and began to talk among themselves. The commandant ordered Ivan Ignatyitch to point the cannon at the group, and he himself applied the match to it. The cannon-ball whistled over their heads without doing any damage. The horsemen dispersed and immediately galloped out of sight, leaving the steppe deserted.

At that moment Vassilissa Yegorovna appeared on

the rampart, accompanied by Masha, who did not wish to be parted from her mother.

'Well?' said the commandant's wife. 'How goes the battle? Where is the enemy?'

'The enemy's not far off,' replied Ivan Kuzmitch. 'God grant that everything will be all right. Well, Masha, are you afraid?'

'No, papa,' replied Marya Ivanovna; 'I should be more afraid alone at home.'

And she looked at me and made an effort to smile. I involuntarily grasped the hilt of my sword, remembering that I had received it from her hands the evening before, as if to defend my beloved. My heart burned. I imagined myself as her knight-protector. I longed to prove that I was worthy of her trust, and waited impatiently for the decisive moment.

At that moment, from behind a rise in the ground about half a verst from the fortress, some fresh groups of horsemen appeared, and soon the steppe was covered by a great number of men, armed with lances and bows and arrows. In the midst of them, on a white horse, rode a man in a red caftan with a drawn sword in his hand; it was Pugachev himself. He stopped; his followers gathered round him and, on his command it seemed, four men broke away from the main body of people and galloped at full speed right up to the fortress. We recognized them as our Cossack traitors. One of them held a sheet of paper above his cap; stuck on the lance of another was the head of Yulai, which was shaken off and hurled over the palisade towards us. The head of the unfortunate Kalmuck fell at the commandant's feet. The traitors cried:

'Don't fire. Come out to the Tsar. The Tsar is here!'

'I'll give it to you!' shouted Ivan Kuzmitch. 'Right, lads – fire!'

Our soldiers fired a volley. The Cossack who held

the letter reeled and fell from his horse; the others
galloped back. I glanced at Marya Ivanovna. Appalled
by the sight of Yulai's bloodstained head and deafened
by the volley, she seemed to have lost her senses. The
commandant summoned a corporal and ordered him
to take the sheet of paper from the dead Cossack. The
corporal went out into the plain and returned, leading
the dead man's horse by the bridle. He handed the
letter to the commandant. Ivan Kuzmitch read it
through to himself and then tore it up into little pieces.
Meanwhile, the rebels seemed to be preparing for
action. Soon the bullets began to whistle about our
ears and several arrows fell close to us, sticking in the
ground and in the palisade.

'Vassilissa Yegorovna,' said the commandant, 'this
is no place for women! Take Masha away; you can see
that the girl is more dead than alive.'

Vassilissa Yegorovna, quietened by the bullets,
glanced at the steppe where much movement could be
observed; then she turned to her husband and said to
him:

'Ivan Kuzmitch, life and death are in God's hands:
give Masha your blessing. Masha, go up to your father.'

Masha, pale and trembling, approached Ivan Kuzmitch, knelt down before him and bowed to the ground.
The old commandant made the sign of the cross over
her three times; then he raised her, and kissing her,
said in a faltering voice:

'Well, Masha, be happy. Pray to God: He will never
abandon you. If you find a good man, may God give
you his love and counsel. Live as Vassilissa Yegorovna
and I have lived. Well, good-bye, Masha. Vassilissa
Yegorovna, take her away as quickly as you can.'

Masha threw her arms round her father's neck and
burst into sobs.

'Let us kiss each other also,' said the commandant's

wife, weeping. 'Good-bye, my Ivan Kuzmitch. Forgive me if I have ever angered you!'

'Good-bye, good-bye, my dear,' said the commandant, embracing his old wife. 'Now, that's enough! Go home now; and if you have time, get Masha to put on a smock.'

The commandant's wife and daughter went away. I followed Marya Ivanovna with my eyes; she glanced back and nodded to me.

Ivan Kuzmitch then turned back to us and fixed all his attention upon the enemy. The rebels gathered round their leader and suddenly began to dismount from their horses.

'Now, stand firm,' said the commandant. 'They're going to attack . . .'

At that moment frightful yells and cries were heard; the rebels were running forward towards the fortress. Our cannon was loaded with grape-shot. The commandant allowed the enemy to come in very close, and then suddenly fired again. The shot fell right in the middle of the crowd. The rebels recoiled on either side and fell back. Their leader was the only one to stay out in front. . . . He was brandishing his sword, and he seemed heatedly to be exhorting the others to follow him. The yells and cries, which had subsided for a moment, were immediately renewed.

'Well, lads,' said the commandant, 'open the gates now and sound the drum. Forward lads, for a sally! Follow me!'

The commandant, Ivan Ignatyitch and I were over the rampart in a twinkling; but the frightened garrison made no move.

'Why do you hold back, children?' cried Ivan Kuzmitch. 'If we've got to die, let us die doing our duty!'

At that moment the rebels rushed upon us and burst into the fortress. The drum fell silent; the garrison threw down their arms; I was hurled to the ground, but

I got up again and entered the fortress with the rebels. The commandant, wounded in the head, stood in the midst of a group of rebels who demanded the keys from him. I was on the point of rushing to his aid when several sturdy Cossacks seized me and bound me with their belts, exclaiming:

'You'll see what'll happen to you, you traitors of the Tsar!'

We were dragged along the streets. The inhabitants came out of their houses, offering bread and salt.* The bells began to ring. Suddenly a cry was taken up among the crowd that the Tsar was awaiting the prisoners in the square and receiving oaths of allegiance. The people thronged towards the square; we also were driven thither.

Pugachev sat in an armchair on the steps of the commandant's house. He was wearing a braided, red Cossack caftan. A tall sable cap with gold tassels was drawn down to his flashing eyes. His face seemed familiar to me. He was surrounded by Cossack elders. Father Gerassim, pale and trembling, stood by the steps with a cross in his hands and seemed silently to be imploring mercy for the forthcoming victims. A gallows was being hastily erected in the square. As we drew near, the Bashkirs drove back the people and presented us to Pugachev. The bells were silent; a deep hush reigned.

'Which is the commandant?' asked the pretender.

Our sergeant stepped out of the crowd and pointed at Ivan Kuzmitch. Pugachev looked menacingly at the old man and said to him:

'How dared you resist me – me, your Tsar?'

The commandant, weakened by his wound, summoned up his remaining strength and answered in a firm voice:

---

* The customary welcome to an honoured visitor.

'You are not my Tsar; you are a thief and an impostor, do you hear?'

Pugachev frowned darkly and waved a white handkerchief. Several Cossacks seized the old captain and dragged him to the gallows. Astride the cross-beam sat the mutilated Bashkir whom we had interrogated the previous day. He held a rope in his hand and a minute later I saw poor Ivan Kuzmitch hanging from the gallows. Ivan Ignatyitch was then brought before Pugachev.

'Swear allegiance,' Pugachev said to him, 'to your Tsar, Pyotr Fyodorovitch!'

'You are not our Tsar,' replied Ivan Ignatyitch, repeating the words of his captain. 'You're a thief and an impostor, my dear man.'

Pugachev again waved the handkerchief and the good lieutenant was hanged beside his old commanding officer.

It was my turn. I looked boldly at Pugachev, ready to repeat the answer of my courageous comrades. Then, to my indescribable astonishment, I saw Shvabrin, his hair cut in peasant style and wearing a Cossack caftan, in the midst of the rebel elders. He went up to Pugachev and said a few words in his ear.

'Hang him!' said Pugachev, without even looking at me.

The noose was thrown round my neck. I began to pray to myself, expressing to God a sincere repentance for all my sins and beseeching Him to keep in safety all those who were close to my heart. I was dragged up to the gallows.

'Don't be afraid, don't be afraid,' repeated my executioners, wishing, in all truth perhaps, to give me courage.

Suddenly I heard a cry:

'Stop, you wretches! Hold!'

The hangman paused. I saw Savyelitch lying at Pugachev's feet.

'Oh, my dear father!' the poor old man was saying. 'What will you gain by the death of this noble child? Set him free: you'll get a good ransom for him; as an example and for the sake of terrifying the others, hang me if you like – an old man!'

Pugachev made a sign and I was immediately unbound and released.

'Our father pardons you,' the rebels said to me.

I could not say at that moment whether I was glad or sorry at my deliverance. My feelings were too confused. I was again brought before the pretender and compelled to kneel at his feet. Pugachev stretched out his sinewy hand to me.

'Kiss his hand, kiss his hand!' said the people around me.

But I would have preferred the most ferocious punishment to such ignoble degradation.

'Pyotr Andreitch, my dear,' whispered Savyelitch, standing behind me and nudging me forward, 'don't be obstinate. What is it to you? Spit and kiss the villain's . . . pfui! . . . kiss his hand!'

I made no movement. Pugachev let his hand drop and said with a smile:

'His Honour seems bewildered with joy. Lift him up!'

I was raised to my feet and set free. I stood watching the continuation of the terrible comedy.

The inhabitants of the fortress began to swear allegiance. They approached one after the other, kissing the cross and then bowing to the pretender. The garrison soldiers were there, too. The regimental tailor, armed with his blunt scissors, cut off their plaits. Then, shaking themselves, they went forward to kiss the hand of Pugachev, who declared them pardoned and received them into his band.

All this went on for about three hours. At last, Pugachev rose from the armchair and, accompanied by his elders, descended the steps. A white horse, richly harnessed, was led up to him. Two Cossacks took him under the arms and placed him in the saddle. He announced to Father Gerassim that he would have dinner at his house. At that moment a woman's scream was heard. Some of the brigands were dragging Vassilissa Yegorovna, stripped naked, and her hair dishevelled, to the steps. One of them had already managed to attire himself in her jacket. The others were carrying off feather-beds, chests, tea-services, linen and chattels of every sort.

'My fathers,' the poor old woman cried, 'spare my life! Kind fathers, take me to Ivan Kuzmitch!'

Suddenly she caught sight of the gallows and recognized her husband.

'Villains!' she cried in a frenzy of rage. 'What have you done to him? Light of my life, Ivan Kuzmitch, my valiant soldier! You were not harmed by Prussian bayonets or Turkish bullets; not on the field of honour have you laid down your life: you have been killed by a fugitive galley-slave!'

'Quieten the old witch!' said Pugachev.

A young Cossack struck her over the head with his sword and she fell dead at the foot of the steps. Pugachev rode off; the crowd rushed after him.

8. An Uninvited Guest

An uninvited guest is worse than a Tartar.

PROVERB

The square was deserted. I was still standing in the same place, unable to collect my thoughts, confused as I was by so many terrible impressions.

Uncertainty as to the fate of Marya Ivanovna tormented me more than anything else. Where was she? What had happened to her? Had she had time to hide? Was her place of refuge safe? Filled with these alarming thoughts, I entered the commandant's house . . . It was completely empty; the chairs, tables and chests had been smashed, the crockery broken and everything else stolen. I ran up the small staircase which led to Marya Ivanovna's bedroom, and for the first time in my life I entered her room. I saw that her bed had been pulled to pieces by the brigands; the wardrobe had been smashed and plundered; the small lamp was still burning before the empty icon-case; the little looking-glass between the windows had survived . . . Where was the mistress of this humble, virginal cell? A terrible thought flashed through my mind: I imagined her in the hands of the brigands . . . My heart sank . . . I wept, bitterly I wept, and loudly called out the name of my beloved . . . At that moment I heard a slight noise and Palashka, pale and trembling, came out from behind the wardrobe.

'Ah, Pyotr Andreitch!' she said, clasping her hands. 'What a day! What horrors . . .!'

'And Marya Ivanovna?' I asked impatiently. 'What had become of Marya Ivanovna?'

'The young lady is alive,' answered Palashka. 'She is hiding at Akulina Pamfilovna's.'

'At the priest's wife's!' I exclaimed in horror. 'My God! Pugachev's there!'

I rushed out of the room, was in the street and tearing headlong to the priest's house in a flash, neither seeing nor feeling a thing. Shouts, bursts of laughter and songs resounded from within. . . . Pugachev was feasting with his comrades. Palashka had followed me there. I sent her to go and fetch Akulina Pamfilovna as quietly as she could. A minute later the priest's wife came to me in the entrance, an empty bottle in her hand.

'For God's sake, where's Marya Ivanovna?' I asked with indescribable agitation.

'The dear girl's lying on my bed, there, behind the partition,' the priest's wife replied. 'A misfortune nearly befell us, Pyotr Andreitch, but thank God, everything went off all right: the villain had only just sat down to dinner when the poor little thing came to and uttered a groan! . . . I nearly died of fright. He heard it and said: "Who's that groaning there, old woman?" I made a very low bow to the thief. "My niece, Tsar; she fell ill about two weeks ago." "And is your niece young?" "She is young, Tsar." "Show me your niece then, old woman." My heart sank within me but there was nothing I could do. "As you wish, Tsar, only the girl's not well enough to get up and come before your Grace." "Never mind, old woman, I'll go and see her myself." And sure enough the wretch went behind the partition; and would you believe it – he actually drew back the curtain and looked at her with his hawklike eyes – but nothing happened . . . God helped us out! But, believe you me, the priest and I were prepared for a martyr's death. Fortunately, the little dear did not know his face. Good Lord above, what things we have lived to see! It can't be denied! Poor Ivan Kuzmitch! Who would have thought it? . . . And Vassilissa Yegorovna? . . . And Ivan Ignatyitch? Why did they kill him? . . . And how did they come to spare you? And what about Alexei Ivanytch Shvabrin? You know he's had his hair cropped in peasant style, and is now feasting with the rebels at our house! He's a sharp one, and no mistake! When I spoke of my sick niece, would you believe it – he looked daggers at me; however, he didn't give me away, and I can be thankful for that.'

At that moment the drunken shouts of the guests and the voice of Father Gerassim were heard. The guests were demanding wine, and the host was calling for his wife. The priest's wife became flustered.

'Go back home, Pyotr Andreitch,' she said. 'I have no time for you now; the villains are drinking themselves under the table. It would be the worse for you if you fell into their drunken hands. Good-bye, Pyotr Andreitch. What is to be, will be; maybe God won't desert us.'

The priest's wife went back into the house. Considerably relieved, I returned to my quarters. As I crossed the square, I saw several Bashkirs assembled around the gallows, dragging the boots off the hanged men's feet; with difficulty I restrained my indignation, feeling that it would be utterly useless to intervene. The brigands were running all over the fortress, looting the officers' quarters. The shouts of the drunken rebels could be heard everywhere. I arrived home. Savyelitch met me on the threshold.

'Thank God!' he cried when he saw me. 'I was beginning to think that the villains had got hold of you again. Well, Pyotr Andreitch my dear, would you believe it – the rogues have robbed us of everything: clothes, linen, our belongings, crockery – there's nothing left. But what of that! Heaven be thanked that you have been spared your life! But did you recognize their leader, master?'

'No, I didn't; who is he, then?'

'What, my dear Pyotr Andreitch? Have you forgotten that drunkard who took your hareskin coat from you at the inn? A brand-new hareskin coat, and the animal burst the seams as he pulled it on!'

I was astonished. Indeed, the resemblance between Pugachev and my guide was striking. I felt sure that Pugachev and he were one and the same person, and now understood why he had spared my life. I could not help but marvel at the strange chain of circumstances: a child's coat given to a tramp had saved me from the hangman's noose, and a drunkard roaming from inn to inn was besieging fortresses and shaking the Government!

'Won't you have something to eat?' asked Savyelitch, his habits unchanged. 'There is nothing in the house, but I'll go out and rummage for something, and prepare it for you.'

Left alone, I became lost in thought. What was I to do? To remain in the fortress occupied by the villain, or to join his band, was unworthy of an officer. Duty demanded that I should go where my service could still be of use to my country in its present critical position . . . But love urged me strongly to stay near Marya Ivanovna and be her defender and protector. Although I foresaw a speedy and inevitable change in the present state of affairs, I trembled at the thought of the danger in which she was.

My reflections were interrupted by the arrival of one of the Cossacks, who ran up to inform me that the 'great Tsar' wished to see me.

'Where is he?' I asked, preparing to obey.

'In the commandant's house,' the Cossack answered.

'Our master went to the bath-house after dinner and now he's resting. Well, your Honour, he is quite clearly a person of distinction: at dinner he was pleased to eat two roast sucking-pigs, and he had his steam-bath so hot that Taras Kurotchkin could not bear it – he had to give the bath-broom to Tomka Bikbayev and only came to when he was doused with cold water. It cannot be denied: his ways are all so dignified . . . And I was told that he showed his Tsar's signs on his chest in the bath-house: on one breast a two-headed eagle the size of a five-copeck piece, and on the other his own likeness.'

I did not consider it necessary to contradict the Cossack's opinion and went with him to the commandant's house, picturing to myself beforehand my meeting with Pugachev, and trying to guess how it would all end. The reader will easily imagine that I did not feel altogether comfortable.

Dusk had begun to fall when I reached the commandant's house. The gallows and its victims loomed black and terrible before me. The body of the poor commandant's wife still lay at the bottom of the steps, where two Cossacks stood on guard. The Cossack accompanying me went in to announce me and, returning at once, led me into the room where, the evening before, I had taken such a tender farewell of Marya Ivanovna.

I was met by an unusual scene. Behind the table, which was covered by a table-cloth and littered with bottles and glasses, sat Pugachev and about ten Cossack elders, wearing hats and coloured shirts, flushed by wine, with purple faces and flashing eyes. Neither Shvabrin nor our sergeant, newly-recruited traitors, were among them.

'Ah, your Honour!' said Pugachev, seeing me. 'You are welcome; come in and take a seat at our table.'

The company moved closer together. I silently sat down at the end of the table. My neighbour, a handsome, well-built young Cossack, filled my glass with some ordinary wine which I did not touch. I began to examine the company with curiosity. Pugachev occupied the seat of honour, his elbows on the table and his broad fist propped against his black beard. His features, which were regular and pleasant enough, had nothing ferocious about them. He frequently turned to a man of about fifty, addressing him sometimes as Count, sometimes as Timofyeitch and sometimes as uncle. All treated each other as comrades, and showed no particular deference to their leader. The conversation turned on the morning's assault, the success of the rising and its future activities. Everyone boasted, advanced his own opinions, and freely contradicted Pugachev. And at this strange council of war it was resolved to march on Orenburg: a bold move and one which was nearly crowned with disastrous success! The march was fixed for the following day.

'Well, lads!' said Pugachev. 'Before we go to bed, let's have my favourite song. Come on, Tchumakov!' *

In a high voice, my neighbour started the following doleful bargeman's song and all joined in the chorus:

Make no sound, mother-forest green,
Do not hinder me, brave lad, from thinking,
For tomorrow I, brave lad, must go before the
   court,
Before the stern judge, before the great Tsar
   himself.
And the great Lord Tsar will begin to question me:
'Tell me, young man, tell me, peasant's son,
With whom you have stolen, with whom you have
   robbed,

* A Yaik Cossack, commander of artillery in Pugachev's army.

And whether you had many companions with you?"
'I will tell you, our hope-true Tsar,
I will tell you the truth, always the truth.
My companions were four in number:
My first companion was the dark night,
My second companion was my knife of damask steel,
My third companion was my good horse,
My fourth companion was my taut bow,
And my messengers were red-hot arrows.'
Then up speaks our hope-true Tsar:
'Praise be to thee, young man, thou peasant's son!
You knew how to steal, you knew how to make
        answer,
And I will therefore make you a present, young
        man –
Of a tall dwelling-house in the midst of a field,
Of two upright posts and a cross-beam above.'

It is impossible to describe the effect that this
peasants' song about the gallows, sung by men already
destined for the gallows, produced upon me. Their
menacing faces, their tuneful voices, the sad expression
they imparted to words already expressive in themselves – all this shook me with some form of mysterious
terror.

Each of the guests drained a last glass, rose from the
table and took leave of Pugachev. I was about to follow
them, but Pugachev said to me:

'Sit down; I want to talk to you.'

We remained facing each other.

For some moments the silence continued between
us. Pugachev looked intently at me, occasionally screwing up his left eye with an extraordinary expression of
foxiness and mockery. At last he burst out laughing
with such unaffected merriment that, as I looked at
him, I began to laugh myself, without knowing why.

'Well, your Honour?' he said to me. 'Confess that you were scared to death when my lads put the rope round your neck. I expect that you were frightened out of your wits. . . . And you would have swung from that cross-beam, had it not been for your servant. I recognized the old grumbler immediately. Well, your Honour, would you have thought that the man who led you to the "umet" was the great Tsar himself?' (Here he assumed an expression of mystery and importance.) 'You are guilty of a serious offence against me,' he continued; 'but I pardoned you for your kindness, and because you did me a service when I was forced to hide from my enemies. But you will see greater things! You will see how I shall reward you, when I take possession of my kingdom! Do you promise to serve me zealously?'

The blackguard's question and his insolence struck me as so amusing that I could not help smiling.

'Why do you smile?' he asked me, frowning. 'Do you not believe that I am the great Tsar? Answer me straight.'

I was confused. I could not acknowledge the tramp as Tsar: to do so would have displayed unpardonable faintheartedness. To call him an impostor to his face would be sentencing myself to death, and that which I was ready to do at the gallows before the eyes of all the people, in the first burst of indignation, now seemed to me as useless boasting. I hesitated. Pugachev awaited my answer in gloomy silence. Finally (and even now I remember the moment with satisfaction), feelings of duty triumphed over human weakness. I replied to Pugachev:

'Listen, I'll tell you the whole truth. Judge for yourself – how can I acknowledge you as Tsar? You are an intelligent man: you would see that I was merely being artful.'

'Who am I, then, in your opinion?'

'God knows; but whoever you are, you're playing a dangerous game.'

Pugachev looked at me quickly.

'Then you don't believe,' he said, 'that I am Tsar Pyotr Fyodorovitch? All right. But is not success for the bold? Did not Grishka Otrepyev* reign in the old days? Think what you like about me, but do not leave me. What is it to you one way or the other? One master's as good as another. Serve me faithfully and truly and I will make you field-marshal and prince. What do you say?'

'No,' I replied firmly. 'I am a nobleman by birth; I have sworn allegiance to my Sovereign Lady, the Empress: I cannot serve you. If you really wish me well, then let me return to Orenburg.'

Pugachev considered.

'And if I let you go,' he said, 'will you at least promise not to serve against me?'

'How can I promise that?' I replied. 'You yourself know that it's not up to me: if I am ordered to march against you, I will – there's nothing for it. You yourself are now a commander; you demand obedience from your men. How would it seem if I refused to serve when my services were needed? My life is in your hands: if you let me go – thank you; if you put me to death – God will be your judge; but I have told you the truth.'

My sincerity struck Pugachev.

'So be it,' he said, slapping me on the shoulder. 'Either put to death or pardon – one or the other. Go where you like and do what you like. Come and say good-bye to me tomorrow, and now go off to bed. I feel quite sleepy myself.'

---

* A monk who claimed to be Dmitri, the son of Ivan the Terrible, who was murdered at the age of nine at Uglitch in 1591. 'False Dmitri' became Tsar in 1605 for less than a year.

I left Pugachev and went out into the street. The night was calm and frosty. The moon and the stars were shining brightly, lighting up the square and the gallows. In the fortress all was still and dark. Only in the tavern was there a light, and from it came the cries of late revellers. I glanced at the priest's house. The shutters and gates were closed. It seemed that all was quiet within.

I arrived back at my quarters and found Savyelitch fretting over my absence. The news of my freedom filled him with unspeakable joy.

'Thanks be to Thee, oh Lord!' he said, crossing himself. 'We will leave the fortress before daybreak tomorrow and follow our noses. I have prepared something for you; eat it up, my dear Pyotr Andreitch, and then sleep safely until the morning.'

I followed his advice and, having eaten my supper with a good appetite, I fell asleep on the bare floor, worn out in mind and body.

9. The Parting

Sweet it was to me, my dear,
To learn to know thee;
Sad, sad it is to part;
As though from my soul I am torn.
    KHERASKOV: *The Parting*

I was awakened by the drum the following morning. I went to the place of assembly. There Pugachev's men were already drawn up around the gallows, where the previous day's victims were still hanging. The Cossacks were on horseback, the soldiers under arms. Flags were flying. Several cannons, among which I recognized ours, were mounted on travelling gun-carriages. All the inhabitants of the fortress were also there, awaiting the pretender. At the steps of the commandant's house, a Cossack was holding a magnificent white Kirghiz horse by the bridle. I sought the body of the commandant's wife with my eyes. It had been moved a little to one side and covered with matting. Pugachev finally appeared at the entrance. The people took off their caps. Pugachev paused at the top of the steps and greeted them all. One of his elders gave him a bag filled with copper coins, which he began to scatter among the crowd by the handful. With cries, the people rushed forward to pick them up, and the affair was not without its casualties. Pugachev was surrounded by his chief accomplices. Shvabrin was among them. Our glances met. In mine he could read contempt, and he turned away with an expression of genuine loathing and affected scorn. Pugachev, catching sight of me in the crowd, nodded and beckoned me to him.

'Listen,' he said to me. 'Set off at once for Orenburg and tell the Governor and all the generals from me that they can expect me within a week. Advise them to receive me with childlike love and obedience; otherwise, they'll not escape a savage death. A pleasant journey, your Honour!'

Then he turned to the crowd and, indicating Shvabrin, he said:

'Here, children, is your new commandant. Obey him in everything; he is answerable to me for you and the fortress.'

I heard these words with horror: with Shvabrin in command of the fortress, Marya Ivanovna would be in his power! Oh God, what would become of her!

Pugachev descended the steps. His horse was brought up to him. He sprang nimbly up into the saddle, without waiting for the Cossacks who were ready to help him mount.

At that moment I saw Savyelitch step out from the crowd; he went up to Pugachev and handed him a sheet of paper. I could not imagine what it was all about.

'What's this?' asked Pugachev importantly.

'Read it and you'll see,' Savyelitch replied.

Pugachev took the paper and examined it significantly for a long time.

'Why do you write so badly?' he said at length. 'My sharp eyes cannot distinguish a single word. Where is my chief secretary?'

A young lad in corporal's uniform ran smartly up to Pugachev.

'Read it aloud,' the pretender said, giving him the paper.

I was extremely curious to know what had prompted my servant to write to Pugachev. In a loud voice the chief secretary began to spell out the following:

'Two dressing-gowns, one cotton and one striped – six roubles.'

'What does this mean?' said Pugachev, frowning.

'Order him to continue,' Savyelitch replied calmly.

The chief secretary went on:

'One uniform of fine green cloth – seven roubles.

'One pair of white cloth breeches – five roubles.

'Twelve holland linen shirts with cuffs – ten roubles.

'One hamper containing a tea-service – two and a half roubles . . .'

'What is this rubbish?' Pugachev interrupted. 'What have I to do with hampers and breeches with cuffs?'

Savyelitch cleared his throat and began to explain.

'This, sir, you will be pleased to see, is an account of those of my master's articles which were stolen by the villains . . .'

'The villains?' Pugachev asked threateningly.

'I beg your pardon: a slip of the tongue,' replied Savyelitch. 'Even if they're not villains, but your lads, they ransacked the place and stole everything. Don't be angry: a horse has four legs and yet it stumbles. Order him to read on to the end.'

'Read on,' said Pugachev.

The secretary continued:

'One chintz bedspread, another of taffeta quilted with cotton wool – four roubles.

'A fox-fur coat covered in crimson flannel – forty roubles.

'Likewise, a hareskin coat given to your Grace at the inn – fifteen roubles.'

'What's this now!' cried Pugachev, his eyes flashing fire.

I confess that I began to fear for the life of my poor servant. He was about to enter into further explanations, but Pugachev interrupted him:

'How dare you intrude upon me with such nonsense?' he cried, snatching the paper from the secretary's hands and throwing it in Savyelitch's face. 'You stupid old man! You've been fleeced: what a misfortune! Why, you old grumbler, you should be eternally praying for me and my lads, and thanking God that you and your master didn't swing from the gallows along with the other traitors . . . Hareskin coat! I'll give you hareskin coat! Why, I'll have your bare skin made into a coat!'

'As you please,' replied Savyelitch, 'but I'm not a free man and must answer for my master's goods.'

Pugachev was evidently in a magnanimous frame of mind. He turned away and rode off without another word to Savyelitch. Shvabrin and the elders followed him. The band set forth from the fortress in orderly fashion. The people moved forward to accompany Pugachev. I stayed behind in the square alone with Savyelitch. My servant was holding his list of my goods in his hands, looking at it with an expression of profound regret.

Seeing that I was on good terms with Pugachev, he had thought to take advantage of it; but his sage intention had not succeeded. I was about to upbraid him for his misplaced zeal, but could not restrain myself from laughing.

'Laugh, master,' Savyelitch answered, 'go on, laugh; but when we have to equip ourselves completely afresh – then we'll see how funny it is.'

I hurried to the priest's house to see Marya Ivanovna. The priest's wife met me with sad news. Marya Ivanovna had developed a strong fever during the night. She lay unconscious and in a delirium. The priest's wife led me to her room. I softly drew near to the bed. The change in her face shocked me. The sick girl did not recognize me. I stood in front of her for a long time, deaf to Father Gerassim and his good wife who, it seemed, were trying to console me. I was agitated by gloomy thoughts. The condition of the poor, defence-less orphan, left alone among ferocious rebels, terrified me, as did my own powerlessness. Shvabrin, Shvabrin more than anything, tortured my imagination. In-vested with power by the pretender, and entrusted with the command of the fortress, where the unhappy girl – the innocent object of his hatred – remained, he was in a position to do anything he wished. What could I do? How could I help her? How could I free her from the villain's hands? There was only one course of action open to me: I decided to leave for Orenburg immediately, in order to speed up the deliverance of the Belogorsky fortress, and if possible, to take a part in the operation. I said good-bye to the priest and Akulina Pamfilovna, warmly entrusting Marya Iva-novna, whom I already considered to be my wife, to their care. I took the poor girl's hand and kissed it, damping it with my tears.

'Good-bye,' the priest's wife said to me, as she accompanied me out of the house. 'Good-bye, Pyotr Andreitch. Perhaps we'll meet again in happier cir-cumstances. Do not forget us and write often. Poor Marya Ivanovna has now no one but you to look to for consolation and protection.'

Going out on to the square, I stopped for a moment, glanced up at the gallows, bowed my head and then left the fortress by the Orenburg road, accompanied by Savyelitch, who had never left my side.

I was walking on, occupied with my thoughts, when suddenly I heard the sound of a horse's hoofs behind me. I looked round and saw a Cossack galloping out of the fortress, holding a Bashkir horse by the bridle and making signs to me from the distance. I stopped and soon recognized our sergeant. Galloping up to us, he dismounted his horse and handing me the bridle of the other, he said:

'Your Honour! Our father wishes you to have this horse and a coat from his own shoulders.' (A sheepskin coat was tied to the horse's saddle.) 'And he also . . .', the sergeant added hesitatingly, '. . . wishes to give you . . . half a rouble . . . but I lost it on the road: be merciful and forgive me.'

Savyelitch looked at him sharply and grumbled:

'Lost it on the road! And what's that clinking under your shirt, you shameless villain?'

'What's that clinking under my shirt?' the sergeant retorted, not in the least put out. 'God be with you, old man! That's the horse's snaffle, and not the half-rouble.'

'All right,' I said, breaking up the argument. 'Give my thanks to him who sent you, and try to find the lost half-rouble on the journey back and keep it for vodka.'

'I'm very grateful, your Honour,' he replied, turning his horse. 'I shall pray for you all my life.'

With these words he galloped back, holding one hand to his shirt, and a minute later, he vanished from sight.

I put on the coat and mounted the horse, Savyelitch taking his seat behind me.

'Well, you can see, master,' said the old man, 'that it was not in vain that I gave that petition to the rogue; the thief's conscience pricked him; even so, this spindle-shanked nag and the sheepskin coat aren't worth half what the rogue stole from us and what you yourself gave him, but you may be able to find some use for them: from a fierce dog, even a tuft of hair.'

10. The Siege of the Town

Pitched in hill and meadow,
From the height, like an eagle he
gazed on the city,
Behind his camp he ordered a rampart
to be built,
In which to hide his thunderbolts,
which he brought by night up to the
city.

KHERASKOV: *Rossiada*

As we approached Orenburg, we saw a crowd of con-
victs with shaven heads and faces disfigured by the
hangman's pincers. They were working near the
fortifications, under the supervision of the garrison
soldiers. Some were carting away the rubbish that had
filled the moat; others were digging up the ground
with spades; on the rampart masons were carrying
bricks and repairing the town wall. Sentries stopped us
at the gates and demanded our passports. As soon as the
sergeant heard that I was from the Belogorsky fortress,
he took me straight to the general's house.

I found the general in the garden. He was inspecting
the apple-trees which had been stripped of their leaves
by the autumn wind and, with the help of an old
gardener, was carefully covering them with warm
straw. His face expressed calm, health and good nature.
He was delighted to see me and began to question me
about the terrible events I had witnessed. I related
everything to him. The old man listened to me attentively as he cut off the dry twigs.

'Poor Mironov!' he said when I had finished my sad
story. 'I feel very sorry: he was a good officer. And
Madame Mironov – she was a fine woman, and what

an expert at pickling mushrooms! But what of Masha, the captain's daughter?'

I replied that she had remained at the fortress, in the care of the priest and his wife.

'Oh dear, oh dear!' observed the general. 'That's bad, very bad. It's quite impossible to rely on the discipline of the brigands. What will become of the poor girl?'

I replied that the fortress was not far away, and that doubtless his Excellency would not delay in dispatching a force of men to rescue its poor inhabitants. The general nodded his head dubiously.

'We shall see, we shall see,' he said. 'We've got plenty of time to discuss that. Do me the pleasure of having a cup of tea with me; a council of war is to be held at my house today. You can give us some trustworthy information concerning this rogue Pugachev and his army. But now go and rest a while.'

I went to the quarters assigned to me, where Savyelitch had already installed himself, and impatiently began to await the appointed time. The reader will easily imagine that I did not fail to make my appearance at the council, which was to have such an influence on my fate. I arrived at the general's at the appointed hour.

I found with him one of the town officials, the director of the customs-house if I remember rightly, a fat, red-faced old man in a brocade coat. He began to question me about the fate of Ivan Kuzmitch, who had been a friend of his, and frequently interrupted me with additional questions and moral observations which, if not showing him to be a man well-versed in the military art, at least indicated that he possessed sagacity and common sense. Meanwhile, the others invited to the council began to assemble.

When everybody had taken his seat and been

handed a cup of tea, the general gave an extremely clear and detailed account of the situation at hand.

'Now gentlemen,' he continued, 'we must decide in what way to oppose these rebels: offensively or defensively? Each of these means has its advantages and its disadvantages. Offensive action holds out greater hope for the quickest possible destruction of the enemy; defensive action is safer and less dangerous . . . And so, let us begin by putting the issue to the vote in the accepted fashion – that is, beginning with the youngest in rank. Mr Ensign,' he continued, addressing me, 'be good enough to give us your opinion.'

I rose and after giving a brief description of Pugachev and his band, I stated firmly that the pretender had not the means to stand up against a force of professional soldiers.

It was clear that my opinion was received by the officials with disfavour. They saw in it the rashness and temerity of a young man. A murmur arose among them, and I distinctly heard the word 'greenhorn' pronounced in a whisper by someone. The general turned to me and said with a smile:

'Mr Ensign, the first votes in councils of war are usually in favour of offensive action; it is as it ought to be. But now let us get on with the voting. Mr Collegiate Councillor, tell us your opinion!'

The old man in the brocade coat hastily finished his third cup of tea, considerably diluted with rum, and answered the general:

'I think, your Excellency, that we should act neither offensively or defensively.'

'How so, Mr Collegiate Councillor?' the general replied, surprised. 'What other tactics are there besides offensive and defensive . . ?'

'Your Excellency, let us proceed by bribery.'

'Ha, ha! Your idea is an extremely sensible one.

Military tactics permit bribery, and we will make use
of your advice. We could promise for the head of this
rogue . . . seventy roubles, or even a hundred . . .
from the secret funds . . .'

'And if,' interrupted the director of the customs-
house, 'and if that doesn't induce these robbers to give
up their leader, bound hand and foot, may I be a
Kirghiz ram, and not a Collegiate Councillor.'

'We will consider it further and discuss it again,' the
general replied. 'We must, however, in any event, take
military measures. Gentlemen, give your votes in the
customary fashion.'

All the opinions were opposed to mine. The officials
spoke of the unreliability of the troops, the uncertainty
of success, the need for caution and so on. All were
agreed that it was more sensible to stay behind strong
stone walls, protected by cannons, than to try the
fortune of arms in the open field. At length, the general, having listened to everyone's opinion, shook the
ashes from his pipe and delivered the following speech:

'Gentlemen, I must state that for my own part I am
in complete accord with the opinion of the ensign,
since his opinion is based on all the rules of sound
military tactics, which are almost always in favour of
offensive rather than defensive action.'

Here he paused and began to fill his pipe. My self-
esteem was triumphant. I cast a proud glance at the
officials, who were whispering among themselves with
an air of displeasure and anxiety.

'But, gentlemen,' he continued, exhaling, together
with a deep sigh, a thick cloud of tobacco smoke, 'I dare
not take upon myself so great a responsibility, when the
affair involves the safety of the provinces entrusted to
me by Her Imperial Majesty, my Most Gracious
Sovereign. And so I fall in with the majority vote,
which has decided that it would be safer and more

sensible to await a siege within the town, and to repel
the enemy's attacks with powerful artillery and (if
possible) by sorties.'

The officials in their turn now glanced scornfully at
me. The council dispersed. I could not but regret the
weakness of this estimable soldier who, contrary to his
own convictions, had decided to follow the advice of
ignorant and inexperienced people.

Some days after this memorable council, we learned
that Pugachev, true to his promise, was approaching
Orenburg. I saw the rebel army from the height of the
town wall. It seemed to me that their numbers had
increased tenfold since the last assault, which I had
witnessed. They now had some pieces of artillery, taken
from the small fortresses Pugachev had conquered.
Recalling the decision of the council, I foresaw a long
confinement within the walls of Orenburg, and nearly
wept with vexation.

I will not describe the siege of Orenburg, which be-
longs to history and has no place in a family memoir. I
will merely say that this siege, due to carelessness on
the part of the local authorities, was disastrous for the
inhabitants, who had to endure hunger and every
possible privation. It is easy to imagine how quite
unbearable life in Orenburg was. Everyone dejectedly
awaited the resolution of his fate; everyone groaned
about the high prices, which were indeed terrible. The
inhabitants grew accustomed to cannon-balls falling in
their courtyards; even Pugachev's assaults no longer
aroused any excitement. I was dying of boredom. Time
wore on. I received no letters from the Belogorsky
fortress. All the roads were cut off. My separation from
Marya Ivanovna was becoming unendurable to me.
Uncertainty as to her fate tortured me. My only
diversion consisted in reconnoitring outside the town.
Thanks to Pugachev, I had a good horse, with which I

shared my meagre ration of food, and on which I daily
left the town to exchange fire with Pugachev's horsemen. In these sorties, the advantage was generally
with the villains who were well-fed, had plenty to
drink and were well-mounted. The emaciated cavalry
from the town was no match for them. On occasions
our hungry infantry also went out into the field; but
the depth of the snow prevented any successful action
against the enemy's scattered horsemen. The artillery
thundered fruitlessly from the height of the rampart,
and once in the field, got stuck, since our horses were
too weak to pull it! And this was what the Orenburg
officials called cautious and sensible!

One day, when we had somehow succeeded in dispersing and driving off a fairly large body of the
enemy, I caught up with a Cossack who had fallen
behind his comrades; I was about to strike him down
with my Turkish sword when he suddenly took off his
cap and cried:

'Greetings, Pyotr Andreitch! How's God treating you?'

I looked at him and recognized our sergeant. I was
delighted beyond words to see him.

'Greetings, Maximytch,' I said to him. 'Is it long
since you left Belogorsky?'

'Not long, Pyotr Andreitch, my dear; I went back
there only yesterday. I have a letter for you.'

'Where is it?' I cried, crimson with excitement.

'I have it here,' answered Maximytch, putting his
hand inside his shirt. 'I promised Palashka that I would
get it to you somehow.'

He then gave me a folded piece of paper and immediately galloped off. I opened it and, with a tremor,
read the following lines:

It has pleased God to deprive me suddenly of both
father and mother: I have no relatives or protectors on

this earth. I turn to you, knowing that you have always wished me well and that you are ready to help any person. I pray to God that this letter may reach you somehow! Maximytch has promised to deliver it to you. Palashka has also heard from Maximytch that he often sees you from a distance in the sorties, and that you take absolutely no care of yourself and do not think of those who pray for you with tears. I was ill for a long time; when I recovered, Alexei Ivanytch, who commands here in place of my late father, forced Father Gerassim to give me up to him, threatening him with Pugachev. I live under guard at our house. Alexei Ivanytch is forcing me to marry him. He says that he saved my life by not exposing Akulina Pamfilovna when she told the villains that I was her niece. But I would rather die than become the wife of such a man as Alexei Ivanytch. He treats me very cruelly and threatens that unless I change my mind and consent, he will take me to the brigands' camp, where, he says, the same will happen to me as happened to Lisaveta Kharlova.* I have asked Alexei Ivanytch to give me time to think. He has agreed to wait three days; if I do not marry him in three days' time, I can expect no mercy from him whatever. My dear Pyotr Andreitch, you are my only protector: save a poor helpless girl! Beseech the general and all the commanders to send us help as soon as possible, and come yourself if you can.

I remain your poor, obedient orphan,

Marya Mironov.

Having read this letter, I nearly went out of my mind. I started back for the town, spurring on my poor

---

* Daughter and wife of fortress commanders in the Orenburg district, both of whom were captured by Pugachev; her father, mother, and husband were executed by Pugachev. She became Pugachev's mistress and was later killed by the rebels.

horse without mercy. On the way I devised one plan after another for the rescue of the poor girl, but could settle on nothing. Galloping into the town, I rode straight for the general's house, and rushed headlong up to him.

The general was walking up and down the room, smoking his meerschaum pipe. He stopped when he saw me. He was doubtless struck by my appearance; he anxiously asked after the reason for my hasty arrival.

'Your Excellency,' I said to him, 'I come to you as to my own father; for God's sake do not refuse me in my request; the happiness of my whole life is involved.'

'What is it, my dear sir?' asked the astonished old man. 'What can I do for you? Tell me.'

'Your Excellency, allow me to take a company of soldiers and fifty Cossacks, and let me free the Belogorsky fortress.'

The general looked at me intensely, doubtless supposing that I had taken leave of my senses (in which he was not far mistaken).

'How? Free the Belogorsky fortress?' he said at last.

'I guarantee success,' I replied with ardour. 'Only let me go.'

'No, young man,' he said shaking his head. 'At such a great distance, the enemy could easily cut off your communications with the main strategic point, and gain a complete victory over you. Your communications severed . . .'

I became alarmed when I saw that he was about to enter into a military discourse, and I hastened to interrupt him.

'The daughter of Captain Mironov,' I said, 'has written me a letter; she asks for help; Shvabrin is forcing her to marry him.'

'Really? Oh, that Shvabrin is a great rascal, and if he falls into my hands, I'll have him tried within twenty-four hours, and we'll shoot him on the fortress parapet! But meanwhile we must have patience . . .'

'Have patience!' I cried, beside myself. 'But meanwhile he marries Marya Ivanovna! . . .'

'Oh!' retorted the general. 'That won't be such a bad thing: it would be better for her, in the meantime, to be Shvabrin's wife: he could then show her his protection; and then, when we shoot him, God willing, suitors will be found for her. Pretty widows don't stay single for long; I mean that a young widow will find a husband quicker than an unmarried girl.'

'I would rather die,' I said in a fury, 'than give her up to Shvabrin!'

'Oho!' said the old man. 'Now I understand: it seems that you're in love with Marya Ivanovna. Oh, that's quite another matter! Poor fellow! But all the same, I cannot give you a company of soldiers and fifty Cossacks. Such an expedition would be mad; I cannot take the responsibility for it.'

I hung my head; despair took possession of me. Suddenly a thought flashed through my mind: what it was, the reader will discover in the following chapter, as the old-fashioned novelists say.

11. The Rebel Camp

At that time the lion was replete, and,
although by nature he is ferocious,
He asked kindly: 'What has pleased you
to come to my den.'   SUMAROKOV

I left the general and hastened to my own quarters.
Savyelitch met me with his customary admonitions.

'What satisfaction can you get out of fighting these
drunken outlaws? Is such the occupation of a nobleman? You never know what may happen: you may
lose your life for nothing. It would be all right if you
were fighting the Turks or the Swedes, but it would be
a sin even to mention the lot you're fighting at the
moment!'

I interrupted him with a question:

'How much money have we got altogether?'

'There's enough for you,' he replied with a satisfied
expression. 'In spite of the rebels' rummaging about,
I managed to hide some.'

And with these words he drew from his pocket a
long knitted purse filled with silver.

'Well, Savyelitch,' I said to him, 'give me half of it
now, and keep the rest for yourself. I am going to the
Belogorsky fortress.'

'Pyotr Andreitch, my dear!' said my good old servant
in a trembling voice. 'Have fear of God; how can you
travel in times like these, when all the roads are
swarming with outlaws! Have pity on your parents,
even if you have none on yourself. Where do you
want to go? And why? Wait a little while: the troops
will soon be here, and they'll catch the rebels; and
then you can go wherever you like.'

But I had fully made up my mind.

'It's too late to argue now,' I answered the old man. 'I must go; I cannot not go. Don't grieve, Savyelitch; God is merciful; perhaps we shall see each other again! And don't have any scruples about the money, but spend it as you will. Buy whatever you want, even if it's three times as expensive as usual. This money I give to you. If I am not back after three days . . .'

'What are you saying, master?' Savyelitch interrupted me. 'That I should let you go alone! Don't imagine that. If you have quite decided to go, I will follow you; even if I have to go on foot I will not leave you. That I should sit behind a stone wall without you! Do you suppose that I've taken leave of my senses? Do as you please, master, but I'll not leave you.'

I knew that it was pointless to argue with Savyelitch, and I allowed him to prepare for the journey. Half an hour later, I mounted my good horse and Savyelitch a lean, limping nag, which one of the inhabitants of the town had given to him for nothing, as he no longer had the means with which to feed it. We reached the gates of the town; the sentries let us through and we left Orenburg.

It was beginning to grow dark. My way led past the village of Berda, one of Pugachev's haunts. The straight road was covered with snow; but the imprint of horses' hooves, daily renewed, could be seen all over the steppe. I rode at a fast trot. Savyelitch could scarcely keep up with me, and kept calling out:

'Slower, master, for God's sake, slower! My accursed nag cannot keep up with your long-legged devil. What's the hurry? It would be all very well if we were going to a feast, but we're more likely going to our deaths. I fear . . . Pyotr Andreitch! . . . Pyotr Andreitch, my dear! . . . Don't destroy me! . . . Good Lord above, the master's child will surely perish!'

The lights of Berda soon began to sparkle. We approached the ravines which formed the natural fortifications of the village. Savyelitch was still with me, never ceasing his plaintive entreaties. I was hoping to go round the village without being observed, when suddenly I saw five peasants, armed with clubs, right in front of me in the darkness. It was the advance guard of Pugachev's camp. They challenged us. Not knowing the password, I wanted to ride past them without saying a word; but they immediately surrounded me and one of them seized my horse by the bridle. I took hold of my sword and struck the peasant over his head; his cap saved him, but he stumbled and the bridle fell from his hands. The others became confused and fled; I took advantage of this moment, spurred on my horse and galloped off.

The darkness of the approaching night might have saved me from any further danger, but suddenly turning round, I saw that Savyelitch was no longer with me. The poor old man had not been able to gallop away from the brigands on his lame horse. What was I to do? After waiting for a few moments and assuring myself that he really was caught, I turned my horse about and went back to rescue him.

Approaching the ravine, I heard noise, cries and my Savyelitch's voice in the distance. I rode faster and soon found myself once more among the peasant sentries who had stopped me a few minutes before. Savyelitch was with them. They had dragged the old man off his nag and were preparing to tie him up. They were delighted at my arrival. They threw themselves upon me with shouts and dragged me off my horse in a twinkling. One of them, apparently the leader, announced that he was going to take us before the Tsar immediately.

'And our father,' he added, 'will be able to decide

whether you be hanged now or whether we should wait until dawn.'

I did not resist; Savyelitch followed my example and the sentries led us away in triumph.

We crossed the ravine and entered the village. Lights were burning in all the huts. Noise and shouting resounded everywhere. I met a large number of people in the street; but no one noticed us in the darkness, and I was not recognized as an officer from Orenburg. We were taken straight to a hut which stood at a corner where two streets met. Several wine-casks and a couple of cannons stood at the gate.

'Here is the palace,' said one of the peasants; 'we'll announce you immediately.'

He went into the hut. I glanced at Savyelitch; the old man was making the sign of the cross and saying a prayer to himself. I waited for a long time; at last the peasant returned and said to me:

'Come inside; our father has given orders for the officer to be taken before him.'

I went into the hut, or the palace as the peasants called it. It was lit by two tallow candles and the walls were covered with gold paper; otherwise, the benches, the table, the hand-basin on a cord, the towel hanging on a nail, the oven-fork in the corner and the wide hearth piled up with cooking-pots – all were the same as in any other cottage. Pugachev was sitting beneath the icons in a red caftan and a tall cap, his arms importantly akimbo. Several of his chief confederates were standing near him with expressions of feigned servility on their faces. It was evident that the news of the arrival of an officer from Orenburg had aroused considerable curiosity among the rebels, and that they had prepared to meet me with pomp. Pugachev recognized me at first glance. His assumed importance immediately vanished.

'Ah, your Honour!' he said to me in a lively way. 'How are you? What's brought you here?'

I replied that I was travelling on personal business and that his people had stopped me.

'And what is your business?' he asked me.

I did not know how to reply. Pugachev, supposing that I was reluctant to explain myself before witnesses, turned to his comrades and ordered them to leave the room. All obeyed with the exception of two, who did not move from their places.

'You can say what you like in front of them,' Pugachev said to me; 'I keep nothing secret from them.'

I glanced out of the corner of my eye at the pretender's confidants. One of them, a puny, bent old man with a grey beard had nothing remarkable about him except for a blue ribbon which he wore across the shoulder of his grey overcoat. But in all my life I shall never forget his companion. He was a tall, corpulent, broad-shouldered man who seemed to me to be about forty-five. A thick red beard, brilliant grey eyes, a nose without nostrils and reddish scars upon his forehead and cheeks gave his broad, pock-marked face an indescribable expression. He wore a red shirt, a Kirghiz robe and Cossack trousers. The first (as I afterwards learned) was a deserter, Corporal Beloborodov, the second, Afanassy Sokolov (nick-named Khlopusha), an exiled convict who had three times escaped from the mines in Siberia. Despite the exceptional feelings of agitation that filled my mind, the company in which I so unexpectedly found myself strongly aroused my imagination. But Pugachev brought me to myself by repeating his question:

'Speak; on what business did you leave Orenburg?'

A strange thought entered my head; it seemed to me that providence, by leading me for a second time to

Pugachev, was giving me an opportunity to fulfil my intention. I made up my mind to take advantage of it and without waiting to consider my decision, I replied to Pugachev's question:

'I was going to the Belogorsky fortress to rescue an orphan who is being persecuted there.'

Pugachev's eyes glittered.

'Which of my people dares to persecute an orphan?' he cried. 'Be he as wise as Solomon, he will not escape my judgement. Speak: who is guilty?'

'Shvabrin is guilty,' I replied. 'He is holding against her will the girl whom you saw ill at the priest's wife's, and wishes to marry her by force.'

'I'll show Shvabrin!' Pugachev said menacingly. 'He'll find out what it means to act on his own and persecute the people when I am master. I'll hang him.'

'Allow me to say a word,' said Khlopusha in a hoarse voice. 'You were in a hurry to appoint Shvabrin as commandant of the fortress, and now you're in a hurry to hang him. You have already offended the Cossacks by putting them under the authority of a nobleman; do not now alarm the noblemen by hanging them at the first accusation.'

'They should neither be pitied nor favoured,' said the old man with the blue ribbon. 'To hang Shvabrin would be no great misfortune; and neither would it be amiss to give this officer a regular questioning: why has he decided to pay us a call? If he does not acknowledge you as Tsar, he cannot appeal to you for justice; if he does acknowledge you as Tsar, why has he been with your enemies in Orenburg until now? Will you not order him to be taken to the prison-office, and there have a fire prepared for him: I reckon that his Grace has been sent here by the Orenburg commanders.'

The old villain's logic seemed pretty convincing to

me. My flesh began to creep at the thought of whose hands I was in. Pugachev observed my perplexity.

'Well, your Honour?' he said to me with a wink. My field-marshal seems to be talking sense. What do you think?'

Pugachev's mockery gave me back my courage. I replied calmly that I was in his hands, and that he could do with me as he wished.

'Good,' said Pugachev. 'Now tell me, how are things in your town?'

'Thank God,' I replied, 'everything's all right!'

'All right?' repeated Pugachev. 'With the people dying of hunger!'

The pretender spoke the truth; but from duty to my oath of loyalty, I began to assure him that these were idle rumours, and that there was enough of every sort of provision at Orenburg.

'See,' broke in the little old man; 'he's deceiving you to your face. All the fugitives unanimously declare that there is famine and sickness in Orenburg, that they're eating carrion there, and think themselves lucky for that; but his Grace assures us that there is plenty of everything. If you want to hang Shvabrin, then hang this young fellow on the same gallows, and then neither will be jealous of the other.'

The accursed old man's words seemed to cause Pugachev to hesitate. Fortunately, Khlopusha began to contradict his comrade.

'That's enough, Naumitch,' he said to him. 'You would do nothing but strangle and cut throats. What sort of a hero are you? To look at you, it's a mystery what keeps your soul in. You've got one foot in the grave yourself, and yet you want to destroy others. Haven't you enough blood on your conscience?'

'What sort of a saint are you?' retorted Beloborodov. 'Where do you get this compassion from?'

'Of course, I have sinned, too,' replied Khlopusha, 'and this arm' (he clenched his bony fist and pushing back his sleeve, revealed a hairy arm) 'and this arm is guilty of shedding much Christian blood. But I have killed my enemy, not my guest; on the highway at the cross-roads or in a dark wood, not at home, sitting behind the stove; with a club or an axe, not with an old woman's slander.'

The old man turned away and muttered the words: 'Slit nostrils! . . .'

'What are you muttering, you old grumbler?' cried Khlopusha. 'I'll give you "slit nostrils"; you wait, your time will come; God willing, you'll smell the hangman's pincers . . . And, in the meantime, watch out that I don't tear your beard off!'

'Generals!' said Pugachev haughtily. 'That's enough of your quarrelling. It wouldn't matter if all the Orenburg dogs were hanging by their legs from the same cross-beam; but it's a bad thing if our own begin to snap at each other's throats. Now make it up between yourselves.'

Khlopusha and Beloborodov did not utter a word and looked darkly at one another. I saw the necessity of changing a conversation which could end very unpleasantly for me, and, turning to Pugachev, I said to him with a jocular expression:

'Oh, I almost forgot to thank you for the horse and the sheepskin coat! If it hadn't been for you, I would never have reached the town, but would have frozen to death on the road.'

My strategy succeeded. Pugachev brightened up.

'One good turn deserves another,' he said, winking and screwing up his eye. 'Tell me now, why are you interested in this girl whom Shvabrin is persecuting? Is she the darling of your heart, eh?'

'She is betrothed to me,' I answered Pugachev,

seeing a favourable change in the weather and no longer finding it necessary to conceal the truth.

'Your betrothed!' cried Pugachev. 'Why didn't you say so before? We'll marry you and have a feast at your wedding!'

Then, turning to Beloborodov:

'Listen, field-marshal! His Honour and I are old friends; let's sit down and have supper together; we'll sleep on it: we shall see what we'll do with him tomorrow.'

I would gladly have escaped the proposed honour, but there was no escaping it. Two young Cossack girls, daughters of the owners of the cottage, covered the table with a white table-cloth, brought in some bread, fish-soup and several bottles of wine and beer, and for the second time I found myself at the same table as Pugachev and his gruesome associates.

The orgy of which I was an involuntary witness lasted far into the night. Finally, intoxication began to overcome the three companions. Pugachev went to sleep, sitting in his place; his comrades stood up and gave me the sign to leave him. I went out with them. On Khlopusha's orders, a sentry took me to the prison-office, where I found Savyelitch and where we were locked up together. My servant was so stunned by all that had occurred that he did not ask me a single question. He lay down in the dark and sighed and groaned for a long time; at last he began to snore, and I gave myself over to reflections which prevented me from sleeping a wink throughout the entire night.

Pugachev summoned me to him the following morning. I went to him. A sledge, drawn by three Tartar horses, stood by the gate. A crowd had gathered in the street. I met Pugachev at the entrance to the cottage; he was dressed for the road, in a cloak and a Kirghiz cap. His companions of the previous evening stood round him with an appearance of servility which strongly contrasted with all that I had witnessed the evening before. Pugachev greeted me gaily and ordered me to take my seat beside him in the sledge.

We sat down.

'To the Belogorsky fortress!' said Pugachev to the broad-shouldered Tartar who was driving the *troika*.

My heart beat violently. The horses began to move, the little bell pealed and the sledge flew off . . .

'Stop! Stop!' cried a voice which was all too familiar to me, and I saw Savyelitch running towards us.

Pugachev ordered the driver to stop.

'Pyotr Andreitch, my dear!' cried my old servant. 'Don't abandon me in my old age among these ras . . .'

'You old grumbler!' Pugachev said to him. 'So God has ordained that we should meet again. Well, get up on the box.'

'Thank you, Tsar, thank you, my dear father!' said Savyelitch as he sat down. 'May God give you a hundred years of good health for protecting and reassuring me, an old man. All my life I will pray for you, and I'll never mention the hareskin coat again.'

The reference to the hareskin coat might have made Pugachev extremely angry. Fortunately, the pretender either did not hear or paid no heed to the inapt remark. The horses galloped off; the crowd in the street stopped and bowed low to the pretender, who nodded his head to both sides. A minute later, we had left the village and were racing over the smooth road.

It is easy to imagine what I felt at that moment. Within a few hours I would be seeing her whom I already thought to be lost to me. I imagined the moment of our reunion . . . I also thought of that man in whose hands my fate lay and who, by a strange chain of circumstances, had become mysteriously connected with me. I recalled the thoughtless cruelty and

the bloodthirsty habits of the man who had volunteered to rescue my beloved! Pugachev did not know
that she was the daughter of Captain Mironov; the
enraged Shvabrin might reveal everything to him;
Pugachev might discover the truth in some other way
. . . And then what would become of Marya Ivanovna?
A cold shudder ran through my whole body and my
hair stood on end . . .

Suddenly Pugachev broke into my reflections,
turning to me with a question:

'What are you so pensive about, your Honour?'

'How could I be otherwise than pensive?' I answered
him. 'I am an officer and a nobleman; yesterday I was
fighting against you, and today I am riding at your
side in the same sledge, with the happiness of my whole
life depending upon you.'

'And what of it?' asked Pugachev. 'Are you afraid?'

I replied that, having been spared by him once already,
I hoped not only for his mercy but even for his help.

'And you're right, by God, you're right!' the
pretender said. 'You saw how my men looked askance
at you; and this morning, the old man again insisted
that you were a spy, and said that you should be
tortured and then hanged; but I did not agree,' he
added, lowering his voice so that Savyelitch and the
Tartar should not hear him, 'since I remembered your
glass of wine and the hareskin coat. You see, I'm not
as bloodthirsty as your brethren say I am.'

I remembered the taking of the Belogorsky fortress,
but I did not consider it necessary to dispute the point
and made no reply.

'What do they say about me at Orenburg?' asked
Pugachev after a pause.

'They say that it'll be difficult to get the better of
you; there's no denying, you've made yourself felt.'

The pretender's face expressed satisfied vanity.

'Yes!' he said gaily. 'I don't fight badly. Do you people in Orenburg know of the battle of Yuzeyeva?* Forty generals killed, four armies taken into captivity. What do you think: d'you think the King of Prussia could rival me?'

The brigand's boasting amused me.

'What do you think yourself?' I asked him. 'D'you think you could beat Frederick?'†

'Fyodor Fyodorovitch? But why not? I've beaten your generals and they've beaten him. Up to now my arms have been successful. Given time, you'll see me march on Moscow!'

'And do you propose to march on Moscow?'

The pretender thought for a while and then said softly;

'God knows. My scope is limited. My men have got their own ideas. They are robbers. I have to keep a sharp look-out: at the first reverse they'll save their heads at the expense of my head.'

'That's just it,' I said to Pugachev. 'Wouldn't it be better to cut loose from them, in good time, and then throw yourself on the mercy of the Empress?'

Pugachev smiled bitterly.

'No,' he replied. 'It's too late for me to repent. There'll be no mercy for me. I will continue as I have begun. Who knows? Perhaps I'll succeed. Grishka Otrepyev reigned over Moscow, didn't he?'

'But you know what happened to him in the end? He was thrown from a window, torn to pieces, burned, and his ashes used to fire a cannon!'

'Listen,' said Pugachev with a sort of wild inspiration. 'I'll tell you a story, which was told to me in my

* A village some 20 miles from Orenburg where, on 9 November 1773, Pugachev inflicted a heavy defeat on Government forces sent to relieve Orenburg.
† Frederick II (the Great) of Prussia (1712–86).

childhood by an old Kalmuck* woman. The eagle once asked the raven: "Tell me, raven-bird, how is it that you live in this bright world for three hundred years, while I only live for thirty-three in all?" "Because, dear eagle", the raven answered, "you drink live blood and I live off carrion". The eagle thought: "I'll give it a try and live off the same food as the raven." Very well. Good. The eagle and the raven flew off. After a time they caught sight of a dead horse and they flew down and alighted upon it. The raven began to peck at it and was well pleased. The eagle tasted it once, once more, shook his beak and said to the raven: "No, brother raven, rather than live off carrion for three hundred years, I would prefer to drink live blood, and then trust to God!" What do you think of the Kalmuck woman's story?'

'Ingenious,' I replied. 'But in my opinion to live off murder and robbery is the same as pecking at carrion.'

Pugachev looked at me with astonishment and made no reply. We both became silent, each of us absorbed in his own thoughts. The Tartar began to sing a sad song; Savyelitch, dozing, swayed on the box. The sledge flew along the smooth winter road. . . . Suddenly I saw a little village on the steep bank of the Yaik, with its palisade and belfry, and a quarter of an hour later, we entered the Belogorsky fortress.

* Buddhist Mongol race of Central Asia who invaded Russia in the sixteenth and seventeenth centuries and settled along the lower Volga.

12. The Orphan

As our little young apple-tree
Has neither branches nor a leafy top,
So our young princess
Has neither father nor mother.
No one to prepare her for life,
No one to bless her.

WEDDING SONG

The sledge drew up in front of the commandant's house. The people had recognized Pugachev's little bell and ran after us in a crowd. Shvabrin met the pretender on the steps. He was dressed as a Cossack and had grown a beard. The traitor helped Pugachev to climb down from the sledge, expressing, in abject terms, his delight and zeal. On seeing me, he became confused; but he quickly recovered himself and stretching out his hand to me, he said:

'Are you one of us? About time, too!'

I turned away from him and made no reply.

My heart ached when we found ourselves in the long, familiar room where the diploma of the late commandant still hung on the wall, as a sad epitaph of the past. Pugachev sat down on the same sofa on which Ivan Kuzmitch, lulled by the scolding of his wife, used to doze. Shvabrin himself brought some vodka. Pugachev drained his glass and, pointing at me, he said:

'Pour his Honour a glass, too.'

Shvabrin approached me with his tray; but for the second time I turned away from him. He did not seem to be himself. With his usual intelligence, he had of course guessed that Pugachev was not pleased with him. He cowered before him and glanced at me distrustfully. Pugachev made inquiries about the situation in the fortress, and reports concerning the enemy's troops and so on, and then suddenly and unexpectedly, he said:

'Tell me, brother, who is this young girl you've got locked up here? Show her to me.'

Shvabrin went as pale as death.

'Tsar,' he said in a trembling voice, '. . . she is not locked up . . . she is ill . . . she is in bed.'

'Take me to her,' the pretender said, getting up from his place.

To refuse was impossible. Shvabrin led Pugachev to Marya Ivanovna's bedroom. I followed them.

Shvabrin stopped on the stairway.

'Tsar!' he said. 'You have power to ask of me what you wish; but do not order a stranger to enter my wife's bedroom.'

I shuddered.

'So you're married!' I said to Shvabrin, ready to tear him to pieces.

'Silence!' interrupted Pugachev. 'This is my affair. And you,' he continued, turning to Shvabrin, 'stop trying to be smart and putting on all these airs and graces; whether she be your wife or not, I wish to be taken to her. Your Honour, follow me.'

At the door of the room Shvabrin stopped again and said in a faltering voice:

'Tsar, I should warn you that she is delirious and has been raving incessantly for the last three days.'

'Open the door!' said Pugachev.

Shvabrin began to search through his pockets and said that he had not brought the key up with him. Pugachev kicked the door with his foot; the lock gave way; the door opened and we entered the room.

I looked and was struck dumb with horror. On the floor, in a tattered peasant's dress, sat Marya Ivanovna, pale, thin, her hair dishevelled. Before her stood a pitcher of water covered with a piece of bread. Seeing me, she started and cried out. I do not remember what I felt at that moment.

Pugachev looked at Shvabrin and said with an ironical smile:

'A nice hospital you've got here!' Then, going up to Marya Ivanovna: 'Tell me, my dear, what is your husband punishing you for? In what way have you offended him?'

'My husband!' she repeated. 'He is not my husband. I will never be his wife! I would rather die, and I will die, unless I am delivered.'

Pugachev looked menacingly at Shvabrin.

'And you dared to deceive me!' he said to him. 'Do you know, you scoundrel, what you deserve?'

Shvabrin fell on his knees. . . . At that moment contempt stifled within me all feelings of hate and anger. The sight of a nobleman at the feet of a fugitive Cossack filled me with disgust. Pugachev softened.

'I'll forgive you this time,' he said to Shvabrin; 'but the next time you commit an offence, I shall take this into account.'

He then turned to Marya Ivanovna and said to her kindly:

'Go, my pretty girl; I give you your freedom. I am the Tsar.'

Marya Ivanovna glanced quickly at him and guessed that the murderer of her parents stood before her. She covered her eyes with both her hands and fell senseless to the ground. I rushed up to her; but at that moment, my old friend Palashka very boldly entered the room and began to attend to her young mistress. Pugachev left the room, and the three of us went down into the drawing-room.

'Well, your Honour!' Pugachev said, laughing. 'We have rescued the fair maiden! What do you say to

sending for the priest and having him marry you to his niece! If you like, I'll be her father by proxy and Shvabrin can be best man, and then we shall feast and drink, without allowing ourselves to be disturbed!'

What I had feared now occurred. Shvabrin, on hearing Pugachev's suggestion, went out of his mind with fury.

'Tsar!' he cried in a frenzy. 'I am guilty; I have lied to you; but Grinev has also deceived you. The girl is not the local priest's niece; she is the daughter of Ivan Mironov, who was hanged at the capture of the fortress.'

Pugachev fixed me with his fiery eyes.

'What does this mean?' he asked, perplexed.

'Shvabrin has told you the truth,' I replied firmly.

'You did not tell me,' remarked Pugachev, whose face became clouded.

'Judge for yourself,' I answered him: 'could I have declared in front of your men that Captain Mironov's daughter was still alive? They would have torn her to pieces. Nothing would have saved her!'

'That's true enough!' said Pugachev, laughing. 'My drunkards would not have spared the poor girl. My good friend, the priest's wife did well to hoodwink them.'

'Listen,' I continued, seeing that he was in a good mood. 'I don't know what to call you, and I don't wish to know . . . But God is my witness that I would gladly repay you with my life for what you have done for me. Only do not demand of me anything which is against my honour or my Christian conscience. You are my benefactor. End as you have begun: let me go away with that poor orphan wherever God may lead us. And wherever you may be and whatever may happen to you, we will pray every day for the salvation of your sinful soul . . .'

It seemed that Pugachev's harsh soul had been touched.

'All right, as you say!' he said. 'Either punish or pardon – one or the other: that's my custom. Take your beauty with you: take her where you want and may God give you love and advice!'

Then he turned to Shvabrin and ordered him to give me a safe-conduct for all the outposts and fortresses that were subject to his command. Shvabrin, utterly defeated, stood as if turned to stone. Pugachev set off to inspect the fortress. Shvabrin accompanied him; I remained behind under the pretext of wishing to prepare for my departure.

I ran up to Marya Ivanovna's bedroom. The door was locked. I knocked.

'Who's there?' asked Palashka.

I pronounced my name. The gentle voice of Marya Ivanovna was heard from behind the door.

'Wait, Pyotr Andreitch. I am changing my dress. Go to Akulina Pamfilovna's; I'll be there presently.'

I obeyed her and went to the house of Father Gerassim. He and his wife ran out to meet me. Savyelitch had already warned them of my coming.

'Greetings, Pyotr Andreitch,' said the priest's wife. 'So God has ordained that we should meet again. How are you? There hasn't been a day we haven't talked about you. And Marya Ivanovna, poor soul, what she has had to endure without you! . . . But tell me, my dear, how you manage to get on so well with Pugachev? Why hasn't he done away with you? That's something to be thankful to the villain for.'

'That's enough chatter, mother,' interrupted Father Gerassim. 'Don't bubble over with everything you know. There's no salvation in too much talking. Pyotr Andreitch, my dear, come in, I beg of you! It's a long, long time since we've seen each other.'

The priest's wife gave me to eat all the food she had

in the house. In the meantime she talked incessantly. She related to me how Shvabrin had forced them to hand over Marya Ivanovna to him; how Marya Ivanovna had wept and had not wished to be parted from them; how Marya Ivanovna had kept in constant touch with them through Palashka (a quick-witted girl who had made the sergeant dance to her tune); how she had advised Marya Ivanovna to write a letter to me, and so on. I in my turn briefly related my tale. The priest and his wife crossed themselves when they heard that Pugachev knew of their deception.

'The strength of the Cross is with us!' said Akulina Pamfilovna. 'May God let the cloud pass over. Well done, Alexei Ivanytch! He's a fine fellow and no mistake!'

At the same moment the door opened and Marya Ivanovna entered the room with a smile on her pale face. She had taken off her peasant's dress and was attired, as before, simply and charmingly.

I seized her hand and for a long time could not utter a single word. We were both silent from fullness of heart. Our hosts felt that they were not wanted and left us. We were alone. Everything else was forgotten. We talked and talked and could not say enough. Marya Ivanovna related to me all that had happened to her since the taking of the fortress; she described to me the full horror of her position, and all the ordeals she had suffered at the hands of the odious Shvabrin. We recalled former happy times . . . We were both weeping . . . Finally, I began to tell her of my proposals. For her to remain at the fortress, subject to Pugachev and under the command of Shvabrin, was impossible. So was the idea of going to Orenburg, which was then enduring all the privations of siege. She had not a single relative in the world. I suggested that she should go to my parents in their village. At first she hesitated; she was afraid, knowing of my father's disapproval. I allayed her anxiety. I knew that my father would consider it both a pleasure and a duty to take in the daughter of a distinguished soldier who had been killed in the service of his country.

'Dear Marya Ivanovna!' I said to her finally. 'I look upon you as my wife. Miraculous circumstances have united us for ever: nothing on earth can separate us.'

Marya Ivanovna listened to me simply, with no false modesty or fanciful pretence. She felt that her fate was tied to mine. But she repeated that under no circumstances would she become my wife without the consent of my parents. I did not oppose her. We kissed passionately, sincerely – and in this way everything was decided between us.

An hour later, the sergeant brought me my safe-conduct, signed with Pugachev's scrawl, and told me that Pugachev wished to see me. I found him ready to set off on his journey. I cannot describe what I felt on parting with this terrible man, this outcast, this villain to all but myself alone. Why not speak the truth? At that moment, I felt strongly drawn to him. I fervently wished to take him away from the environment of the criminals he commanded, and to save his head while there was still time. Shvabrin and the people who crowded round us prevented me from expressing all that filled my heart.

We parted friends. Pugachev, seeing Akulina Pamfilovna in the crowd, raised a threatening finger at her and winked significantly; he then took his seat in the sledge, ordered the driver to make for Berda and, as the horse began to move, leaned once more out of the sledge and cried out to me:

'Farewell, your Honour! Perhaps we'll meet again sometime.'

Indeed we did see each other again, but in what circumstances! . . .

Pugachev was gone. For a long time I stood gazing at the white steppe over which his *troika* glided away. The crowd dispersed. Shvabrin disappeared. I returned to the priest's house. Everything was prepared for our departure; I did not wish to delay any longer. All our belongings had been packed into the commandant's old carriage. The drivers harnessed the horses in a flash. Marya Ivanovna went to say farewell to the graves of her parents, who had been buried behind the church. I wanted to accompany her, but she begged me to let her go alone. She returned a few minutes later, silently weeping. The carriage was drawn up. Father Gerassim and his wife came out on to the steps. The three of us – Marya Ivanovna, Palashka and I – took our seats inside. Savyelitch climbed up on to the box.

'Good-bye, Marya Ivanovna, my little darling! Good-bye, Pyotr Andreitch, my dear!' said the priest's wife. 'A good journey, and may God give happiness to you both.'

We set off. I saw Shvabrin standing at the little window of the commandant's house. His face expressed gloom and wickedness. I had no wish to triumph over a defeated enemy and turned my eyes in another direction. At last we passed through the fortress gates and left the Belogorsky fortress for the last time.

13. The Arrest

Do not be angry, Sir; according to my duty
I must send you to prison at this very
*   moment.*
– As you please, I am ready; but I hope
That you will allow me to have my say
*   first.*

KNYAZHNIN

United so unexpectedly with the dear girl about whom I had been so desperately worried that very morning, I could not trust myself and imagined that everything that had happened to me was an empty dream. Marya Ivanovna gazed pensively, now at me, now at the road, and it seemed that she had not yet fully come to herself. We were silent. Our hearts were too tired. The time slipped by unnoticed, and a couple of hours later we found ourselves at the next fortress, which was also held by Pugachev. Here we changed horses. The speed with which they were harnessed and the servile helpfulness of the bearded Cossack who had been put in command of the fortress by Pugachev, showed that, thanks to our driver's loquacity, I was welcomed as one of their master's more powerful favourites.

We set off again. Dusk was beginning to fall. We drew near to a small town where, according to the bearded commandant, we would find a strong detachment on its way to join the pretender. We were stopped by the sentries. To the challenge: 'Who goes there?' the driver replied in a loud voice: 'A friend of the Tsar with his wife.'

Suddenly a crowd of Hussars surrounded us, uttering the most terrible curses.

'Come out, friend of the devil!' said the moustached

sergeant to me. 'We'll make things pretty hot for you and your little wife!'

I stepped down from the sledge and demanded to be taken to their commanding officer. On seeing an officer, the soldiers stopped swearing. The sergeant took me to the major. Savyelitch never left my side, muttering to himself:

'So much for your being a friend of the Tsar! Out of the frying pan into the fire . . . Good heavens above, how will all this end?'

The sledge followed us at walking pace.

Five minutes later, we arrived at a small, brightly-lit house. The sergeant left me under guard and went in to announce me. He returned at once and informed me that his Excellency had no time to see me, but had ordered that I be taken to the prison, and my wife to him.

'What does this mean?' I exclaimed in a rage. 'Has he gone out of his mind?'

'I don't know, your Honour,' replied the sergeant. 'Only his Excellency ordered that your Honour should be taken to prison, and that her Honour be brought to his Excellency, your Honour!'

I dashed up the steps. The guards did not think of holding me back and I ran straight into the room where six Hussar officers were playing cards. The major was dealing. Imagine my astonishment when, glancing up at him, I recognized Ivan Ivanovitch Zurin, who had once fleeced me at the Simbirsk inn!

'Is it possible?' I cried. 'Ivan Ivanytch! Is it really you?'

'Well, well, well! Pyotr Andreitch! What good wind brings you here? How are you, brother? Would you care to join in the game?'

'Thank you, but I would rather you gave orders for quarters to be found for me.'

'What do you want with quarters? Stay with me.'

'I cannot; I am not alone.'

'Well, bring your comrade along too.'

'I am not with a comrade; I am . . . with a lady.'

'With a lady! Where did you pick her up? Aha, brother!'

With these words Zurin whistled so expressively that everyone burst out laughing, and I became thoroughly confused.

'Well,' continued Zurin, 'so be it. You shall have quarters. But it's a pity . . . We might have had a spree as before . . . Hey, boy! Why don't they bring along Pugachev's lady friend? Or is she being obstinate? Tell her that there's nothing to be frightened about, that the gentleman's very nice and won't harm her – and then bring her in by the scruff of her neck.'

'What are you saying?' I said to Zurin. 'What lady friend of Pugachev's? It is the daughter of the late Captain Mironov. I rescued her from captivity and am now taking her to my father's village where I shall leave her.'

'What! So it was you who was announced just now? Gracious me, what does this mean?'

'I'll tell you later. But now for God's sake, set the poor girl at rest, whom your Hussars have frightened out of her wits.'

Zurin immediately made the necessary arrangements. He went out into the street himself to apologize to Marya Ivanovna for the involuntary misunderstanding, and ordered the sergeant to take her to the best quarters in the town. I stayed to spend the night with him.

We had supper, and when we were alone together, I told him of my adventures. Zurin listened most attentively.

When I had finished, he shook his head and said:

'That's all very well, brother; one thing is not, however: why the devil do you want to get married? As an officer and a man of honour, I have no wish to deceive you, but take it from me that marriage is all rubbish. Why take on all the trouble of a wife and be for ever fussing over children? Have done with the scheme. Listen to me: rid yourself of this captain's daughter. I have cleared the road to Simbirsk and it's now quite safe. Send her off on her own to your parents tomorrow, and you yourself stay in my detachment. There's no reason why you should go back to Orenburg. If you fall into the rebels' hands again, you might not be able to get away from them so easily a second time. In this way your foolish infatuation will die of its own accord and all will be well.'

Although I did not altogether agree with him, I did feel that duty and honour demanded my presence in the Empress's army. I decided to follow Zurin's advice: to send Marya Ivanovna to my father's village, and to stay on in his detachment.

Savyelitch came in to help me undress; I told him to be ready the next day to continue the journey with Marya Ivanovna. He began to hedge.

'What, master? Why should I desert you? Who's going to look after you? What will your parents say?'

Knowing how obstinate my servant was, I decided to persuade him by kindness and sincerity.

'My dear friend, Arkhip Savyelitch,' I said to him, 'do not refuse me, but be my benefactor; I do not need a servant here and I would not feel easy if Marya Ivanovna were to continue her journey without you. By serving her, you will be serving me, since I have firmly resolved to marry her as soon as circumstances allow it.'

At this Savyelitch threw up his arms with a look of indescribable astonishment.

'To marry!' he repeated. 'The child wants to marry. But what will your father say, and what will your mother think?'

'They will give their consent, they will give their consent for sure,' I replied, 'when they know Marya Ivanovna. But I rely upon you. My father and mother have confidence in you; you will put in a good word for us, won't you?'

The old man was touched.

'Oh, Pyotr Andreitch, my dear,' he replied, 'although it's early for you to start thinking of marriage, Marya Ivanovna is such a good young lady that it'd be a sin to miss the opportunity. Let it be as you wish! I will accompany her, the angel, and tell your parents respectfully that such a bride does not need a dowry.'

I thanked Savyelitch and lay down to sleep in the same room as Zurin. My mind was in a state of great turmoil and I began to chatter. Zurin was willing enough to converse with me at first; gradually, however, his words became less frequent and more disconnected; finally, instead of replying to one of my questions, he began to snore and make whistling noises. I stopped talking and soon fell asleep myself.

I went round to Marya Ivanovna the following morning. I informed her of my proposals. She admitted their good sense and at once agreed with me. Zurin's detachment was to leave the town that same day. There was no time to be lost. I said good-bye to Marya Ivanovna there and then, entrusting her to the care of Savyelitch and giving her a letter to my parents. Marya Ivanovna burst into tears.

'Good-bye, Pyotr Andreitch!' she said in a soft voice. 'Whether we shall get the chance to see each other again, God alone knows; but never in my life shall I forget you; till my dying day, you alone shall remain in my heart.'

I could not reply to her. We were surrounded by
people. I did not wish to give way before them to the
feelings that agitated me. Finally she departed. I
returned to Zurin, silent and dejected. He tried to
cheer me up; I wanted to be distracted; we spent the
rest of the day in a noisy and riotous fashion, and set
out on our march in the evening.

It was now near the end of February. Winter, which
had made military operations difficult, was drawing to
its close, and our generals were preparing for con-
certed action. Pugachev was still besieging Orenburg.
Meanwhile our detachments were joining forces
around him and moving in on the villains' nest from
all sides. The rebellious villages were restored to
obedience at the sight of our troops; brigand bands
everywhere fled from us, and everything gave promise of a speedy and successful conclusion of the
campaign.

Shortly afterwards, Prince Golitsin had defeated*
Pugachev beneath the walls of the fortress of Tatish-
cheva, dispersed his followers, relieved Orenburg and,
it seemed, had struck the final and decisive blow to the
rebellion. Zurin was at this time sent against a band
of rebellious Bashkirs, who dispersed before we ever
reached them. Spring found us in a little Tartar
village. Rivers overflowed and roads became im-
passable. We consoled ourselves in our inaction with
the thought that this tedious and trivial war against
brigands and savages would soon come to an end.

But Pugachev had not been captured. He showed up
in the industrial areas of Siberia, where he collected
fresh bands of rebels and again began to perpetrate
his acts of villainy. Once more reports of his successes
were spread abroad. We heard of the destruction of the
Siberian fortresses. Soon, news of the capture of

* On 22 March 1774.

Kazan* and the pretender's intention to march on Moscow alarmed the army leaders, who had been slumbering in the care-free hope that the despised rebel was utterly powerless. Zurin received orders to cross the Volga.

I will not describe our campaign and the conclusion of the war. I will only say that the distress became extreme. We passed through villages laid waste by the rebels, and had of necessity to requisition from their poor inhabitants what they had somehow succeeded in saving. Administration everywhere came to a stop; the landowners hid themselves in the forests. Bands of brigands ransacked the countryside; commanders of individual detachments punished and pardoned as the fancy took them; the condition of the whole vast area where the conflagration raged was terrible. . . . God forbid that we should ever see a Russian rebellion – so senseless and merciless – again!

Pugachev was in flight and being pursued by Ivan Ivanovitch Mikhelson.† We soon heard of his complete defeat. At last Zurin received news of the capture of the pretender and, with it, the order to halt. The war was over. At last I could go to my parents! The thought of embracing them and of seeing Marya Ivanovna, of whom I had received no news at all, filled me with delight. I danced about like a child. Zurin laughed and said with a shrug of the shoulders:

'No, you'll come to a bad end! Once married, you're lost!'

But in the meantime a strange feeling poisoned my joy: the thought of the villain, smeared with the blood

---

* On 12 July 1774; town on Volga some 450 miles east of Moscow and some 100 miles north of Simbirsk.
† General (1740–1807), responsible for Pugachev's final defeat near Tsaritsin (now Volgograd, previously Stalingrad) in August 1774.

of so many innocent victims, and of the execution awaiting him, involuntarily troubled me.

'Emelya, Emelya,' I thought with vexation, 'why didn't you throw yourself on a bayonet, or get hit by grape-shot? It would have been the best thing you could have done.'

How could I think otherwise? The thought of him was inseparable from the thought of the mercy he had shown to me at one of the most terrible moments of my life, and of the deliverance of my bride from the hands of the hateful Shvabrin.

Zurin granted me leave of absence. In a few days I would be among my family again, would be seeing Marya Ivanovna once more . . . An unexpected storm suddenly burst upon me.

On the day appointed for my departure, at the very moment I was preparing to start on my journey, Zurin came to me in my quarters, holding a paper in his hand and looking exceedingly troubled. Something pricked my heart. I was frightened without knowing why. He sent my orderly away and announced that he had something to tell me.

'What is it?' I asked anxiously.

'A minor unpleasantness,' he replied, handing me the paper. 'Read what I have just received.'

I began to read it: it was a secret order to all detachment commanders to arrest me, wherever I might be, and to send me at once under guard to Kazan, to the committee of inquiry established to investigate the Pugachev Rising.

The paper nearly fell from my hands.

'It can't be helped!' said Zurin. 'My duty is to obey orders. No doubt reports of your friendly journeys with Pugachev have somehow reached the authorities. I hope that the affair will have no serious consequences and that you will be able to clear yourself before the committee. Don't be depressed, and set off at once.'

My conscience was clear; I had no fear of the tribunal; but the thought of deferring, perhaps for several months, the sweet moment of reunion daunted me. Zurin bade me a friendly farewell. I took my seat in the open cart. Beside me sat two Hussars with drawn swords, and I drove off along the high road.

14. The Tribunal

Popular rumour is like a sea-wave.
PROVERB

I was convinced that my unwarranted absence from
Orenburg was the only reason for my arrest. I could
easily justify myself: sallying out against the enemy
had not only never been forbidden, but had even been
most forcefully encouraged. I could be accused of
excessive rashness, but not of disobedience. My friendly
relations with Pugachev, however, could be proved by
a number of witnesses and would appear, at the very
least, extremely suspicious. Throughout the whole of
the journey I thought of the interrogation that was
awaiting me and considered the answers that I should
make, and resolved to tell the complete truth at the
tribunal, believing that this would be the simplest and,
at the same time, the surest means of justification.

I arrived at Kazan, which had been devastated and
set on fire. Instead of houses, one saw heaps of burnt
wood and blackened walls without roofs or windows.
Such were the traces left by Pugachev! I was conducted to the fortress, which had remained intact in the
midst of the burnt-out town. The Hussars handed me
over to the officer of the guard. He ordered a black-
smith to be sent for. Chains were put round my legs
and shackled tightly together. I was then taken to the
prison and left alone in a narrow, dark cell with blank
walls and a small iron-barred window.

Such a beginning did not augur well for me. However, I lost neither courage nor hope. I had recourse to
the consolation of all those in affliction, and, after having tasted the sweetness of prayer for the first time,

poured out from a pure but tortured heart, I fell into a peaceful sleep, not caring about what might happen to me.

The next morning the gaoler awoke me with the announcement that my presence was required at the committee of inquiry. Two soldiers conducted me through the courtyard to the commandant's house and, stopping in the front hall, sent me into the inner room on my own.

I entered a fairly large room. At a table, which was covered with papers, sat two men: an elderly general, who looked cold and severe, and a young captain of the Guards of about twenty-eight, with a very pleasant appearance and a free and easy manner. At a separate table near a little window sat a secretary with a pen behind his ear, bent over a piece of paper, ready to record my evidence.

The interrogation began. I was asked my name and profession. The general inquired whether I was the son of Andrei Petrovitch Grinev. To my reply, he retorted sternly:

'A pity that such a worthy man should have such an unworthy son!'

I replied calmly that whatever the accusations levelled against me might be, I hoped to refute them by a frank expression of the truth. My assurance did not please him.

'You are sharp, my friend,' he said to me, frowning; 'but we've seen your type before!'

Then the young man asked me under what circumstances and at what time I had entered Pugachev's service, and on what missions I had been employed by him.

I replied indignantly that, as an officer and a nobleman, I could never have entered Pugachev's service, or accepted any missions from him.

'How is it then,' retorted my interrogator, 'that this nobleman and officer was the only one to be spared by the pretender, when all his comrades were villainously murdered? How is it that this same officer and nobleman feasted with the rebels as a friend and received presents – a sheepskin coat, a horse and half a rouble – from the leader of the rebels? How did such a strange friendship come about and on what was it founded, if not on treachery, or, at least, on base and criminal cowardice?'

I was deeply offended by the words of the officer of the Guards and heatedly began to justify myself. I related how my acquaintanceship with Pugachev had begun in the steppe, at the time of the storm; how, at the capture of the Belogorsky fortress, he had recognized me and spared me. I admitted that I had no scruples about accepting the sheepskin coat and the horse from the pretender; but I also said that I had defended the Belogorsky fortress against the villain to the last extremity. Finally I referred to my general, who could testify to my zeal at the time of the calamitous siege of Orenburg.

The stern old man took up an opened letter from the table and began to read it aloud:

In answer to your Excellency's inquiry concerning Ensign Grinev, who is accused of being involved in the present disturbance and of entering into communication with the villain, contrary to the regulations of the Service and the oath of allegiance, I have the honour to say that the same Ensign Grinev was in service at Orenburg from the beginning of October of last year, 1773 until 24th February of this present year, on which date he absented himself from the town, and since then has not appeared again under my command. It was heard from deserters that he was in Pugachev's camp and that

*he went with him to the Belogorsky fortress, where he
had been garrisoned before; as regards his conduct, I
can only . . .*

Here he broke off his reading and said to me
severely:

'What do you say for yourself now in justification?'

I was about to continue as I had begun and explain
my connection with Marya Ivanovna as openly as the
rest of what I had said. Suddenly, however, I felt an
overwhelming revulsion. It occurred to me that if I
mentioned her name, the committee would demand
her appearance at the inquiry; and the thought of
involving her name with the hateful denunciations of
the villains and of herself being obliged to confront
them – this terrible thought so appalled me that I
faltered in my speech and became confused.

My judges, who seemed at first to listen to my
answers with a certain goodwill, again became prejudiced against me at the sight of my confusion. The
officer of the Guards demanded that I be brought face
to face with my principal accuser. The general gave
orders for 'yesterday's villain' to be brought in. I
turned quickly towards the door, awaiting the appearance of my accuser. A few minutes later, to the rattling
of chains, the door opened and into the room came –
Shvabrin. I was astonished at the change in his
appearance. He was terribly thin and pale. His hair,
not so long ago as black as soot, was now quite grey; his
long beard was tousled. He repeated his accusations in a
weak but determined voice. According to him, I had
been sent by Pugachev as a spy to Orenburg; every day
I used to ride out on sallies with the purpose of trans-
mitting written information about all that had
occurred in the town; finally I had openly gone over to
the pretender, had accompanied him from fortress to

fortress, trying to bring about the ruin of my fellow-traitors so as to take over their positions and profit by the rewards handed out by the pretender.

I listened to him in silence and was pleased at one thing alone: the name of Marya Ivanovna had not been mentioned by the odious villain, either because his vanity could not bear the thought of one who had spurned him with contempt, or because there lay hidden in his heart a spark of the same feeling which had forced me to keep silent – whichever it was, the name of the daughter of the commandant of the Belogorsky fortress was not uttered in the presence of the committee. I became still more confirmed in my intention to keep her name out of the proceedings, and when the judges asked me what I had to say in refutation of Shvabrin's evidence, I replied that I was sticking to my original statement and had nothing further to say in justification of myself.

The general ordered us to be taken away. We left the room together. I glanced calmly at Shvabrin but did not say a word to him. He smiled maliciously at me and, lifting up his chains, hastened past me. I was taken back to the prison and was not required for a further interrogation.

I was not a witness to all that now remains for me to tell the reader; but I have heard it related so often that the smallest details are engraved upon my memory, and it seems to me as if I had been invisibly present.

Marya Ivanovna was received by my parents with that sincere hospitality which distinguished people of a past age. They regarded it as a divine blessing that they had been afforded the opportunity of sheltering and giving a warm welcome to the poor orphan. They soon became sincerely attached to her, since it was impossible to know her and not love her. My love no longer appeared as mere folly to my father, and my mother wished for only one thing – that her Petrusha should marry the captain's pretty daughter.

The news of my arrest came as a shock to my family. Marya Ivanovna had related the story of my friendship with Pugachev so simply to my parents, that not only had they not worried about, but had even been forced to laugh often at the whole affair. My father would not believe that I had been involved in the infamous rebellion, whose aim it was to overthrow the throne and exterminate the nobles. He questioned Savyelitch closely. My servant did not conceal the fact that I had been a guest of Emelyan Pugachev and that the villain had shown me favour; but he swore that he had heard no word of any treason. My old parents were reassured and impatiently began to await favourable news. Marya Ivanovna was greatly alarmed, however, but she kept silent, for she was given in the highest degree to modesty and prudence.

Several weeks passed . . . Suddenly my father received a letter from our relative in Petersburg, Prince B**. The prince wrote to him about me. After the usual compliments, he informed him that the suspicions concerning my participation in the rebels' designs had unhappily proved to be only too well-founded, that capital punishment would have been meted out to me as an example to others had not the Empress, in consideration of my father's faithful services and declining years, decided to spare his criminal son and, commuting the ignominious death sentence, to exile him to a remote part of Siberia for life.

This unexpected blow nearly killed my father. He lost his customary strength of character and his grief (normally silent) poured out in bitter complaints.

'What!' he used to repeat, beside himself. 'My son

participated in Pugachev's designs! Blessed Lord, that
I should have lived to see this! The Empress spares
him from the death penalty! Does that make it any
better for me? It's not the death sentence that's so
terrible: my great-grandfather's grandfather died upon
the scaffold in defence of that which his conscience
regarded as sacred; my father suffered together with
Volinsky and Khrushchev.* But that a nobleman
should betray his oath of allegiance, should associate
with brigands, with murderers and fugitive serfs! . . .
Shame and disgrace upon our name! . . .'

Frightened by his despair, my mother did not dare
to weep in his presence and tried to cheer him up by
speaking of the uncertainty of rumour and the unreliability of other people's opinions. My father was
inconsolable.

Marya Ivanovna suffered more than anybody. Being
certain that I could have justified myself if only I had
wished, she guessed at the truth and held herself
responsible for my misfortune. She concealed her tears
and suffering from everyone, all the while thinking of
means by which to save me.

One evening my father was sitting on the sofa,
turning the pages of the 'Court Calendar'; but his
thoughts were far away, and the reading of the 'Calendar' did not produce its usual effect upon him. He was
whistling an old march. My mother was silently
knitting a woollen vest, and from time to time a tear
would drop on her work. Suddenly Marya Ivanovna,
who was also in the room, sitting at her work, declared
that it was absolutely essential that she should go to

* A. P. Volinsky (1689–1740) and A. F. Khrushchev (1691–1740)
– a minister in the government of Anna Ioannovna and his assistant – were convicted of attempting to place Elizabeth, the daughter of Peter the Great, upon the throne, and executed in June
1740.

Petersburg, and she begged my parents to provide her with the means to go. My mother was very upset.

'Why do you want to go to Petersburg?' she said. 'Can it be, Marya Ivanovna, that you too wish to forsake us?'

Marya Ivanovna replied that her whole future depended upon this journey and that she was going in search of protection and help from influential people, as the daughter of a man who had suffered for his loyalty.

My father lowered his head: every word that reminded him of the alleged crime of his son was hurtful to him and seemed as a bitter reproach.

'Go, my dear!' he said to her with a sigh. 'We don't want to stand in the way of your happiness. God grant you an honest man for a husband, and not a discredited traitor.'

He stood up and left the room.

Marya Ivanovna, left alone with my mother, in part explained her plan. My mother embraced her with tears and prayed for the successful outcome of her scheme. Marya Ivanovna was fitted out and, a few days later, she set out on her journey with the faithful Palashka and the faithful Savyelitch who, forcibly separated from me, consoled himself with the thought that at least he was serving my betrothed.

Marya Ivanovna arrived safely at Sofia, * and learning that the Court was then at Tsarskoye Selo, she resolved to stop there. A small recess behind a partition was assigned to her at the posting-station. The stationmaster's wife immediately fell into conversation with her and informed her that she was the niece of one of the stove-tenders at the Court, and initiated her into all the mysteries of Court life. She told her at what hour the Empress usually awoke, when she drank her

* Posting-station and small town near Tsarskoye Selo (now Pushkin), summer residence of the Russian Imperial family.

coffee and when she went out for a walk; which great
lords were then with her; what she had been pleased
to say at table the previous day, whom she had received
in the evening – in a word, Anna Vlassyevna's conversation was worth several pages of historical memoirs
and would have been a precious contribution to
posterity.

Marya Ivanovna listened to her attentively. They
went into the grounds of the Palace. Anna Vlassyevna
told her the story of every alley and every little bridge
and, having strolled about as long as they wished, they
returned to the posting-station, very pleased with each
other.

Early the next morning, Marya Ivanovna woke,
dressed and went quietly into the Palace grounds. It
was a beautiful morning; the sun lit up the tops of the
linden trees, already turning yellow under the cool
breath of autumn. The broad lake glittered motion-
lessly. The swans, only just awake, came sailing
majestically out from under the bushes which over-
hung the banks. Marya Ivanovna walked towards a
beautiful lawn where a monument had just been erected
in honour of Count Pyotr Alexandrovitch Rumyant-
sev's* recent victories. Suddenly a little white dog of
English breed ran barking up towards her. Alarmed,
Marya Ivanovna stopped in her tracks. At the same
moment she heard a pleasant female voice saying:

'Don't be frightened; it doesn't bite.'

And Marya Ivanovna saw a lady sitting on the bench
opposite the monument. Marya Ivanovna sat down at
the other end of the bench. The lady looked at her
intently; Marya Ivanovna, in her turn, by throwing
several sidelong glances, managed to examine her from
head to foot. She was wearing a white morning-gown,

* 1725–95; one of the greatest generals of the time of the Empress
Catherine II.

a night-cap and a jacket. She seemed to be about forty. Her full, rosy face expressed dignity and calm, and her blue eyes and slight smile had indescribable charm. The lady was the first to break the silence.

'Doubtless you are a stranger here?' she said.

'Yes, ma'am; I only arrived here yesterday from the country.'

'You came with your parents?'

'No, ma'am, I came alone.'

'Alone! But you're still so young.'

'I have neither father nor mother.'

'I presume you're here on some business or other?'

'Yes ma'am; I have come to present a petition to the Empress.'

'You are an orphan: I imagine you're complaining of some injustice or injury?'

'No, ma'am. I have come to ask for mercy, and not justice.'

'May I ask who you are?'

'I am the daughter of Captain Mironov.'

'Of Captain Mironov! The same who was commandant of one of the Orenburg fortresses?'

'The same, ma'am.'

The lady was apparently moved.

'Forgive me,' she said in a still kinder voice, 'for interfering in your affairs, but I am often at Court; tell me the content of your petition and I may be able to help you.'

Marya Ivanovna rose and thanked her respectfully. Everything about the unknown lady involuntarily attracted her and inspired her confidence. Marya Ivanovna drew a folded paper from her pocket and handed it to her anonymous protectress, who began to read it to herself.

At first she read with an attentive and benevolent expression; but suddenly her face changed, and Marya

Ivanovna, who was following her every movement with her eyes, was frightened at the severe look on her face, a moment before so pleasant and calm.

'You are pleading for Grinev?' the lady said coldly. 'The Empress cannot pardon him. He sided with the pretender, not out of ignorance and credulity, but as an unprincipled and dangerous scoundrel.'

'Oh, it isn't true!' cried Marya Ivanovna.

'How, not true!' retorted the lady, flushing all over.

'It's not true, in God's name, it's not true! I know all, I'll tell you everything. It was for me alone that he underwent all the misfortunes that have overtaken him. And if he didn't justify himself before the tribunal, it was because he didn't wish to involve me.'

And she related with great ardour all that is already known to my reader.

The lady listened to her attentively.

'Where are you staying?' she asked when Marya Ivanovna had finished speaking; on hearing that she was at Anna Vlassyevna's, she added with a smile: 'Ah, I know! Good-bye, and don't tell anyone of our meeting. I hope that you will not have to wait long for an answer to your petition.'

With these words she rose and walked away down a covered alley, and Marya Ivanovna returned to Anna Vlassyevna's filled with joyous hope.

Her hostess scolded her for going out so early; the autumn air, so she said, was harmful to a young girl's health. She brought in the samovar and was on the point of launching into an endless series of stories about the Court, when suddenly a Palace carriage drew up at the steps and a lackey entered the room with the announcement that the Empress was pleased to summon the daughter of Captain Mironov to her presence.

Utterly amazed, Anna Vlassyevna began to bustle about.

'Gracious me!' she cried. 'The Empress summons you to the Court. How has she got to know about you? And how, my dear, will you present yourself to the Empress? I don't suppose you know even how to walk in Court fashion . . . Hadn't I better come with you? I could at least put you on your guard against some things. And how can you go in your travelling dress? Shall I send to the midwife's for her yellow Court gown?'

The lackey announced that it was the Empress's wish that Marya Ivanovna should go on her own and in the clothes she was wearing. There was nothing for it: Marya Ivanovna took her seat in the carriage and drove off to the Palace, accompanied by the blessings and advice of Anna Vlassyevna.

Marya Ivanovna felt that our fate was about to be decided; her heart beat violently. A few minutes later the carriage stopped at the Palace. Trembling, Marya Ivanovna went up the steps. The doors were flung open before her. She passed through a long series of deserted, magnificent rooms; the lackey led the way. Finally, arriving at a closed door, he said that he would go in and announce her and left her by herself.

The thought of coming face to face with the Empress so terrified her that she could scarcely stand up straight. A minute later the door opened and she entered the Empress's dressing-room.

The Empress was seated at her dressing-table, surrounded by courtiers who respectfully made way for Marya Ivanovna. The Empress turned towards her with a kind smile, and Marya Ivanovna recognized her as the lady with whom she had talked so openly a few minutes previously. The Empress summoned her to her side and said with a smile:

'I am glad to be able to keep my word to you and grant your petition. Your business is settled. I am convinced of the innocence of your betrothed. Here is a letter for your future father-in-law.'

Marya Ivanovna took the letter with a trembling hand and, bursting into tears, fell at the Empress's feet; the Empress raised her up and kissed her.

'I know you're not rich,' she said, 'but I owe a debt to the daughter of Captain Mironov. Do not worry about the future. I shall take it upon myself to look after you.'

After encouraging the poor orphan, the Empress dismissed her. Marya Ivanovna drove away in the same Palace carriage. Anna Vlassyevna, who had been impatiently awaiting her return, overwhelmed her with questions which Marya Ivanovna somehow answered. Anna Vlassyevna, although disappointed at her poor memory, ascribed it to provincial shyness and magnanimously excused her. That same day Marya Ivanovna, without so much as a glance at Petersburg, returned to the country . . .

The memoirs of Pyotr Andreyevitch Grinev end here. It is known from family tradition that he was released from his imprisonment towards the end of the year 1774 by an edict of the Empress; that he was present at the execution of Pugachev, who recognized him in the crowd and nodded to him with his head which, a minute later, was shown lifeless and bleeding to the people. Soon afterwards Pyotr Andreyevitch married Marya Ivanovna. Their descendants still flourish in the province of Simbirsk. About thirty versts from *** there is a village belonging to ten landowners. In one of the wings of the house there can be seen, framed and glazed, a letter written in the hand of Catherine II. It is addressed to Pyotr Andreyevitch's father and contains the justification of his son and praise to the heart and intelligence of the daughter of Captain Mironov.

Pyotr Andreyevitch Grinev's manuscript was given to me by one of his grandchildren, who had heard that I was engaged upon a work dealing with the times described by his grandfather. With the relatives' permission, I have decided to publish it separately, after finding a suitable epigraph for each chapter and after taking the liberty of changing some of the surnames.

19 October 1836 *The Editor*